T0340913

VINTAGE
BLACKENED

Vinoy Thomas hails from Nellikkampoyil, Iritty, in north Kerala. A schoolteacher by profession, he is among the most prominent writers in Malayalam. His short-story collections include *Ramachi*, *Mullaranjanam* and *Adiyormisiha Enna Novel*. His debut novel, *Karikkottakkary* (*Blackened*) was selected as one of the five best novels in a DC Books competition. His second novel, *Puttu* (*Anthill*), won the Kerala Sahitya Akademi Award for the best Malayalam novel of 2021. In 2019, *Ramachi* had won the same award for short stories. Vinoy has also authored a children's book, *Anatham Piriyatham*. He is a gifted scriptwriter and has to his credit a few acclaimed movies. His short stories have also been made into movies.

After completing his master's degree in economics, Nandakumar K. started his career as a sub-editor at *Financial Express*, followed by stints in international marketing and general management in India and abroad. His co-translation of M. Mukundan's *Delhi Gadhakal, Delhi: A Soliloquy*, won the JCB Prize for Literature in 2021. His other translations are: *A Thousand Cuts*, the autobiography of Professor T.J. Joseph; *The Lesbian Cow and Other Stories* by Indu Menon; *In the Name of the Lord*, the autobiography of Sr Lucy Kalappura (*Karthavinte Namathil*); *Anthill* (*Puttu*) and *Elephantam Misophantam* (*Aanaththam Piriyaththam*) by Vinoy Thomas; and *Zin* by Haritha Savithri. Nandakumar is the grandson of Mahakavi Vallathol Narayana Menon. He lives in Dubai and works for a shipping line as a business analyst.

VINOY THOMAS

TRANSLATED BY
NANDAKUMAR K.

Blackened

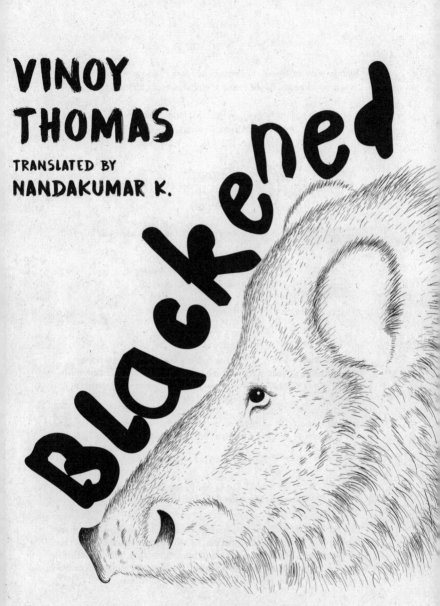

VINTAGE
An imprint of Penguin Random House

VINTAGE

Vintage is an imprint of the Penguin Random House group of companies
whose addresses can be found at global.penguinrandomhouse.com

Published by Penguin Random House India Pvt. Ltd
4th Floor, Capital Tower 1, MG Road,
Gurugram 122 002, Haryana, India

First published in Vintage by Penguin Random House India 2024

Copyright © Vinoy Thomas 2024
Translation copyright © Nandakumar K.
Foreword copyright © S. Hareesh

All rights reserved

10 9 8 7 6 5 4 3 2 1

This is a work of fiction. Names, characters, places and incidents
are either the product of the author's imagination or are used fictitiously,
and any resemblance to any actual person, living or dead, events or
locales is entirely coincidental.

Please note that no part of this book may be used or reproduced in any manner
for the purpose of training artificial intelligence technologies or systems.

ISBN 9780143458654

Typeset in Bembo MT Pro by MAP Systems, Bengaluru, India
Printed at Thomson Press India Ltd, New Delhi

This book is sold subject to the condition that it shall not, by way of trade
or otherwise, be lent, resold, hired out, or otherwise circulated without the
publisher's prior consent in any form of binding or cover other than that in
which it is published and without a similar condition including this condition
being imposed on the subsequent purchaser.

www.penguin.co.in

Foreword

The history of Homo sapiens is a chronicle of migrations and journeys of great permanence or no return. We all have descended from migrants one way or the other. What is uncertain is only the eras in which the journeys happened and the gaps between their timelines. The driving forces were the search for better living conditions, scarcity of resources, evangelism, trade, fascination for exploration and many others. The most recent large-scale migrations have been by Europeans to the American and Australian continents. They turned those lands almost entirely into their own.

Kerala is small strip of land measuring 560 km long and 38,683 square kilometres. Presently, on the global scale, the migrations within this tiny space may seem trivial. However, eighty-five to ninety years ago, it was not so insignificant. It transformed the economic, social and political histories of Kerala.

Two major migrations have taken place in Kerala over the last century. They include the high-range migration to the present-day Idukki district and the Malabar migration to what is now known as north Kerala. The Kerala of today was split into three princely states during those days. Thiruvithamkoor that consisted parts of current-day Tamil Nadu and Kochi which may be called central Kerala, were largely independent states although under British rule. Malabar, which came under the Madras Province of British India, was larger than these two princely states. Malayalam spoken in these three states had significant dialectical differences. Moreover, Kerala, which has forty rivers flowing transverse into the sea, had poor transportation facilities at that time—railway lines were limited and trunk roads practically non-existent.

In both instances, the migrants majorly comprised people from central Travancore. To be more precise, Syrian Christians who were denizens of this region. They revelled in the superiority of their fair complexion, equated themselves with high castes, and emulated Hindus in practising their own brand of casteism. They were hard-working and industrious; and were among the first to benefit from the progress in education that happened in Travancore.

Many reasons encouraged their migration. The first was the increase in population that resulted from the advent of modern medicine. Every Syrian Christian boy considered establishing a family on his own steam and under his sole authority the primary aim of his life. Since the Nair and Nampoothiri communities, prominent in contemporary Kerala society, practised a joint family system, their men had no such ambitions in life. The majority of Ezhavas, the next larger community in numbers, lacked wealth and resources.

The second reason was poverty and privation. The two world wars had destroyed the economy and finances of Travancore. There are those who believe that the famine in the early 1940s killed more people in Travancore than in any other region in India, save Bengal.

The third reason was the misrule in Travancore. Tamil Brahmins ruled the roost as *diwans* of Travancore. The active participation and strong support given by the Christians to the Responsible Governance Movement led by the Travancore State Congress provoked the then diwan, Sir C.P. Ramaswami Iyer. The resultant feeling of insecurity and lack of prospects compelled many to seek greener pastures.

The space of Vinoy Thomas's novels is Malabar, and its threads are the life stories of its first migrants and their descendants. He is himself a scion of migrants from Central Travancore.

Migration transformed Malabar in multiple ways. The migrants brought new farming techniques to the fertile eastern reaches of Malabar. The region lay dormant under the hegemony of the landlord class and the prevalent traditions of a tribal nature. The migrants toiled not to amass wealth but to essentially produce enough food for their families and themselves. The migrant Christians introduced scientific farming in the region. They facilitated and eased the flow of cash money.

All this led to the building of new roads; opening of stores and business outlets; founding of new towns; establishment of schools. The infusion of diverse cultures can awaken a land. However, none of this was facile. They had to fight adverse weather, wild animals and infectious diseases. Many among the initial batches of migrants failed, or succumbed to diseases or forces of nature, or returned home. Others had to face local resistance.

However, many litterateurs and some of the news media looked at this important phase in the state's modern history in a different light or gave it a different spin. This state had long since held a view that literature is not Christians' cup of tea. During those days, burlesque poetry that lampooned a Christian poet as Christian Kalidasa and described him as a water snake in a dry pond was very popular here.

Our country looks down on manual labour. Mainstream literature did two hatchet jobs on migration—one, it ignored migration. That may have been born out of a sentiment that a migrant's life and their life stories do not make for good literature. The reason could be that in the romantic literature that they churned out, manual labour and human survival had no place.

Second, in the rare stories that they figured in, the migrants were tarred with the same brush. This gave rise to the popular saw in Malabar that if one runs into a migrant and a king cobra, one should kill the migrant first. The migrants' love for the land was misrepresented as greed. The term 'migrants' was replaced with 'invaders'. They were accused of destroying the environment and being forest squatters. There were writings that painted migrants and tribals as antagonists of the civil society. Even to this day, mainstream Malayalam literature looks upon migrants as villains. There have been only rare attempts to counter this.

There are many reasons for the evolution of such a narrative. The primary one is the high castes' antipathy towards manual labour. The majority of the writers come from this background. The language of literature was a romantic, high-caste diction. Migrant lives and what this language stood for were like chalk and cheese and did not mix, like oil and water.

A secondary reason was politics. The majority of the migrants were democrats and Congress sympathizers. In the 1940s, communism was the flavour of the month among the denizens of Malabar. The protest at the newcomers from Travancore upending the prevalent systems was another cause of this. Malayalam literature always had a preponderance of leftist sentiments. All the discourse on literature is controlled by left sympathizers. This also led to migration being painted as bad and migrants being demonized.

As an example, the politically driven, ecology-friendly literature presents paddy as a good crop and paddy fields as a beautiful place on the face of the earth. On the other hand, rubber is painted as a commercially driven, evil crop and the rubber plantation as a sinister, malevolent place. There is a simple reason for this—the majority of the plantation owners and workers were Christians. In Malayalam literature, a paddy grower is always a poor, simple-minded farmer, and a rubber grower is an avaricious, money-grubbing philistine.

Works that overturned such narratives have mainly come out of Paul Zacharia who hails from central Travancore. However, his fiction does not spring from or is underpinned by a migrant society. However, Vinoy Thomas's two novels and short stories are deeply rooted in and draw sustenance from the lives of migrants of Malabar. Therefore, his writings are creating many ripples in Malayalam literature.

He underscores that the lives of migrants also make excellent fiction material. He also refutes and debunks the tropes and prejudices that Malayalam literature had engendered so far about migration and migrants. He deconstructs and refurbishes the romanticized literature dished out till now. At the same time, Vinoy does not shy away from mocking and criticizing the migrant's life while being one of them.

Syrian Christians are steadfast in their religious and sectarian beliefs. So is their belief in family values and integrity. We have seen these were an impetus for migration. Vinoy's maiden novel *Karikkottakkary,* translated as *Blackened*, mocks caustically the first belief and lays it bare.

His second novel, *Puttu,* translated as *Anthill,* shakes the foundations of the institution of family. A writer who is politically conscious and who is grounded and does not indulge in self-deception should write this way. He should shatter the prejudices and bigotry that traditional literature has propagated and perpetuated; weave stories from the lives around him. In the same instant, he should hold a mirror up to and castigate it with the insight of an insider.

Karikkottakkary/Blackened and *Puttu/Anthill* are novels that do justice to the lives of migrants by aesthetically chronicling them in the larger context and history of migration. They juxtapose the journeys of the past century that happened in Kerala—which may look trivial now— with the greater and more significant journeys that humans have undertaken over many millennia.

S. Hareesh

Blackened

Prologue

Adhikarathil Family Reunion

The Adhikarathil family was one among the ancient, venerated Christian families of Kerala. The distinctive family history written after considerable research and genealogical studies, under the supervision of M.P. Padmanabha Panicker, underscores this facet of that noble family.

Afroth, the brother of Mar Sapir Iso, the custodian of the Tharisa Church, was the family's progenitor in 842 CE. He hailed from Persia, and as per the royal decree, he married Maninanga, from the Puniyarath Mana, a *nampoothiri tharavad*. The Adhikarathil family sprung from that union.

Venad chieftain Ayyan Adikal Thiruvadikal had granted Syrian Christians seventy-two land grants such as of Thalakkanam, Enikkanam, Meniponnu, Polippennu, Iravuchoru and Kutanazhi. The family name Adhikarathil—which in the vernacular means authority—could have come from these grants.

Whatever it may have been, the family had emerged from the union of two noble lineages, one native and one foreign. This meant that its members were tall and fair.

As one of the pre-eminent families in the history of Christianity in Kerala, in order to protect the tradition of purity of their pedigree and lineage, the Adhikarathil family had laid down a few strict bye-laws:

1. When brides are chosen for the family, their bloodline, going back at least five generations, should be investigated and their family's unblemished nobility should be ascertained.

2. All members should be staunch and steadfast Christians and believers (this was later amended to Roman Catholic Church believers).

3. When girls of the family are to be married off, similar investigations and determinations are required to be done.

4. The members of the Adhikarathil family can have only two occupations—either trading carried out by the progenitor or landownership as practised by the progenitrix.

5. Those who do not abide by these conditions may be expelled from all branches of the family. They shall not have the right to use the Adhikarathil family name.

From time to time, those who failed to honour and abide by these laws and were banished from the family ended up as Adhikarathil Puthenveetil, Adhikarathil Thazhaeppurayil or

Adhikarathil Kozhinjamyaalil families, though none of their members used 'Adhikarathil' as part of their family names.

The official family history claims that members of the Adhikarathil family were found to be involved in all the critical and historical episodes of the Catholic Church in the state. The Synod of Diamper at Udayamperoor, Coonan Cross Oath, the fight against the Puthankoottukar or New Party in the first schism in the Syrian Christian community— at least one member of the Adhikarathil family was present in these episodes.

As long as the sun and moon endure, the Adhikarathil family's predominance should also endure without any diminution. In the opulent quinquennial family unions held with pomp and deep, devout devotion, those present from various generations were reminded of this. Though the early history does touch upon family reunions, it can also be read in the family history that it was systematized, in the manner seen in the present day, around 1870 by Varkeyavira, the hardworking *karanavar* those days and a resident of Uzhavoor in Thiruvithamkoor.

The family members held this forebear's vision in high esteem. One day, in his old age, his walking stick in hand, he headed for his regular stroll. He walked along the foot trails and side lanes. He bent down and picked up an overripe coconut that had brushed against his foot.

'Lord Varkey, this is Pathittethil Pillai's land.'

The landowner's nephew only said so much. For three days, Varkeyavira lay in his armchair on the patio of his house. On the fourth day, he summoned his three sons to his side.

'We have reigned over a whole county. Yet, though it was inadvertent, your father was humiliated. When I walked a mere mile, I lost my way, ended up on someone's land. You are the ones who have to do the walking now. You should not have to step into another man's land. Even if you walk a whole day, it should be only through Adhikarathil lands. For that, Malavar is better.'

The family has on record that those words of Varkeyaviravaliachan set off the migration of the family to Malabar, which helped a large section of the family to prosper.

The sons of Varkeyavira—Pappachan, Kochu and Kuncheriya—had identified for the family, in the valleys of the Western Ghats, locations ranging from Mannarkkad in the south to Sullia in the north. The family grew only plantation crops—rubber, coffee, cardamom, tea, pepper and cashew along with a few annual crops that the family needed for their own consumption.

'Our karanavars' foresight helped us to remain landlords even after those guys' land reforms acts,' is how Adhikarathil Kuncheriya described the family's vision in concentrating only on estates, referring to the Communist government's actions to distribute land among the landless. Occasionally, he would also pass a vain opinion that all the other migrants from Thiruvithamkoor were workers in the Adhikarathil family's estates. He had cornered estates in the region which has today become Kannur and Kasaragod districts.

By the time the valleys became populated, Kuncheriya had become an old man. Kunjepp, his eldest son, was running the show. He had selected Malom, which became the stronghold of the family and built the tharavad there. He made estates for his sons in the neighbourhood. His youngest son, Philippose, lived in the tharavad, and the elder one, Johnny, in another house in Malom.

Kunjepp, more vainglorious than Kuncheriya, abided by the family norms without compromises. The day he came to know that his younger son had made a pass at a maid, he headed for Alakkode to check on a prospective bride for him. With the blessings of his father, Philippose wed Rosamma, the daughter of Valiath Rarichan, the leading grandee of Alakkode. When the union did not produce offspring even after two years, Kunjepp was distressed. He handed a candle to his son and daughter-in-law and advised them, 'Go to Arthunkal, light this candle and pray to Veluthachan. To have a fair son like him.'

Philippose and Rosamma went to Arthunkal, lit the candle and prayed. The next month, Rosamma had morning sickness. Philippose and Kunjepp went back and thanked Veluthachan and lit more candles.

In the ninth month, on 18 May 1972 to be exact, Kunjepp arrived at Josegiri Hospital in Kanhangad bearing a sterling gold ring, sweetmeats, a tin of baby talcum powder and dresses to see his grandson, who lay flush against his mother's belly, enjoying its warmth. After entering the room, he first looked between the tiny legs of the baby. It was, thankfully, a boy.

His dark testicles resembled flecked rubber seeds. As his eyes moved away from the testicles to other parts of the body, his knees turned into jelly. The darkness of the testicles did not end; it spread to the extremities with more virulence. When he realized that this was the kind of dark-skinned brood that had never been born in his family, he had to catch hold of the edge of the chair to keep himself from staggering. He shot a look at Rosamma and left the room without uttering a word.

The baptism was done with little pomp; Kunjepp was not even present at the church. Johnny, his uncle, was the godfather. When asked what he should be christened, Philippose said, 'Eranimos, Eranimos Philippose.'

Johnny was astonished. Whose name was this? There had been no karanavar with that name in their family. Well, anyway, new names are always better.

The relatives, acquaintances and family friends got their first glimpse of the baby on the day of the baptism. They whispered among themselves, 'Hey, this guy is a Karikkottakkaran.'

That was the day Karikkottakkary entered Eranimos's life for the first time. After forty-two years, when he sat down to narrate his amazing history, he gave it the title 'Karikkottakkary'.

Chapter 1

Pannikkalippattu

I have always wondered why my father chose the droll name Eranimos for my christening. It may be that he wanted the dark child of the Adhikarathil family to be easily identified by relatives and acquaintances. Or did he want me to overcome the downsides of my dark skin with a name that would ram itself into everyone's mind? Whatever it may be, my name had a certain ring and rhymed well.

In school, my friends chose my name for their ditties:

Eranimos, Spider-moss,
Gingerly Pincer-moss.

While some sang in this fashion, others brought my dark skin into the mix:

Eranimos, this is the moss,
Like the night, the black moss.

I joined the chorus gladly, happy and proud that my name figured in the parodies. The songs that I sang about myself gradually led me to like songs that had a good rhythm and tempo. Songs that could be sung easily; songs that stayed in the mind when heard once. Those songs were not confined to my school.

The powerful songs came in search of me along the paths I took; among the loggers as they strained to shift the lumber; during the smoke-filled breaks of the estate workers; during the pissing contests, as we stood on a mud wall at the school perimeter.

In the song that Madwoman Narayani sang, as she stood swathed in multiple sarees on the way to our school, Thacholi Othenan was a helpless and virtuous man.

Thacholi Othenan was thrashed by urchins,
Why, didn't he have arms and legs?

Some of the songs were risqué and dangerous. They carried meanings unknown to us and could have got us beaten up.

When, in all my innocence, I sang '*Don't look at this and get turned on, colocasia flower, this one has a lover afore*', I did not know the song was about the phallic flower that was being cautioned by a girl against getting excited by the sight of her vulva as she squatted to pee. I was chased and lashed with a stick broken off the coffee plant by my *appan*. I came to understand the context of the song much later in life.

I became the official singer in my school since I kept singing the lilting, foot-tapping and powerful songs. That I did not have an ear for filmy or devotional songs, nor could I sing them did not trouble me. My songs were like the green sprouts that sprang up after the rains, songs that were rooted in the land . . . songs that had life and grew on people . . . songs that flowered.

As my childhood was spent singing songs, I was oblivious to the ridicule that came my way due to my dark complexion. I paid no attention to the questions people who met me for the first time asked the others in hushed tones. However, in my adolescence, it was a song that made me aware of how humiliating my dark skin was.

The Adhikarathil family's twenty-eighth family reunion—the first one in Malabar—was held in Malom. I was awaiting my results of the tenth standard public examination. My father oversaw all the arrangements. The participants had judged that, though this was the first one in Malabar, it lacked nothing in pomp and grandeur and did not detract from the family's prestige and reputation.

As the priest conducted the rousing Rasa service at the altar of the Malom Church in a devotion-charged atmosphere, a look of justifiable conceit slowly spread on the faces of the grandees of the family. In their own imagination, God's kingdom resembled Kerala. And God, a khadi-wearing popular baron. They also believed that their family did the most to prop up His authority.

After the mass, the family members walked towards St Sebastian's auditorium for the event. The event was not planned with a lot of panache. Since we were traditionally plantation owners and traders, we did not set much store by the imperatives of flow and beauty in cultural events.

One of the better-dressed men used to take up the microphone and welcome the elders to the dais. It was a welcome speech shorn of all formalities. On that day, this was followed by Ulahannan uncle—president of the family reunion committee, held in high esteem by the family and who claimed that he controlled the rubber wholesale business of Kerala—calling out a name to be the next speaker. The first name normally invoked is that of the bishop of the diocese, as was this time too.

In his speech, the bishop extolled the dazzling heritage of the family, our fealty to the Church, and the strong presence we had in Kerala's mercantile space. Those who paid attention to his speech were amazed that the bishop was following our fortunes so closely.

The minister and the MLA did not have much to add to what the prelate had said. They spoke grandly of the emotional support and munificence that our family had extended to their party. They reminded us of the unqualified success that awaited anyone from the family who would choose to join politics.

However, all those who mattered in the family had decided that they would give politics a wide berth. Landowning and commerce were our forte, and that was how it would remain.

After the MLA wound up his speech, unexpectedly, Ulahannan uncle called me to the stage.

'The best singer of the family. The son of Adhikarathil Philippose of Malom, Eranimos.'

As he spoke, the audience clapped heartily. Though everyone in the Malom branch knew me, I was a stranger to the attendees from other branches of the family. They were the ones who clapped with all their heart. When they saw me as I climbed the steps to the stage, the claps faded away quickly to nothing. I got the feeling that they were not expecting a youth with curly hair, dark skin and thick lips. On the dais, I stood by the side of the fair, glowing, tall toffs of the Adhikarathil family like a foreigner.

My cousin Sunny *chettayi*, standing in the front row to the right of the stage, laughed and called out loudly, 'Karikkottakkary.'

The audience around him did not understand the import of what he had said, but the alliteration of *kari*—which in the vernacular means coal—made them break out in giggles as well.

Strangely, that word gave me strength. I decided on the song I should sing. I looked at the audience over the microphone placed in front of me. Swathed in a sea of white, they waited in silence as if inside an incense-filled church. I dissolved the faces of the audience and obliterated the individuals. They all turned into a white patina called the Adhikarathil family.

In my new voice that was on the cusp of breaking and taking on the timbre of an adult male, I said, 'Respected family members, Pannikkali is an art form that is fast losing its roots. I shall sing the theme song of Pannikkali, a form of entertainment that Pulayas of yore performed.

I pay homage to mother, father, guru and the divine,
I recite the tales of the boar reincarnation.
Guru keep me and bless me to perform,
The songs and acts of the boar reincarnation.

Four-legged, stiff-tailed, small-eared,
Curled tusks on either side of the snout.
You mount the tallest of the hills,
Your colours twinkle as you climb.
With a body dark as rain clouds,
You stand on the hilltop and proclaim.

The fruits and berries of the forest,
You dig them up and gobble.
When in the water, immerse yourself
Lap it up, have your fill.

A rogue boar may be the frailest of all,
Your tusks are still fearsome:
Even the serpent shies away from your tusks,
The wolf packs stay away from your tusks.
As you toss up everything with the tusks,
Your form granted to you
Ten times on these hills
Let the hills bloom and the world too bloom.

I was living the song.

Within me the song writhed like earthworms; boars came and stood in front of me.

The smell of loam; the stringy adventitious roots of tubers; the salinity of the sweat pouring off dark skins; the cool interiors of the bamboo huts with *muli* grass thatch; the smoke of the flambeau kept in the middle of the circle of storytellers and their audience; the frothy, loamy mud of the fields into which the feet sunk in till the ankles; waddling ducks nosing through the mud in search of fish . . . the song brimmed over as hundreds of unexperienced emotions.

The audience was with me till I sang the last line. However, when the song ended, the nobility of their births turned them apathetic. In the deafening, insufferable silence, I came down from the stage, my head bowed.

I had, like a culprit, turned into a black boar. Outside the auditorium, I stood under the fig tree like a boar. The word 'Karikkottakkary' uttered by Sunny chettayi before my song rustled overhead, among the leaves.

I had heard the song for the first time in Karikkottakkary. I had gone to watch the north zone tug-of-war tournament being conducted on a new concrete track in the Devamata Church. All the prominent teams of Malabar were present.

The prize for the winning team, a young buffalo bull, stood snorting, tethered to the coconut palm in front of the church. The children crowded around the buffalo which had yellow and white ribbons tied around its neck. The gravedigger Varkey was trying to drive them away waving a single tender palm leaf.

The contestants were led to a shop in the market, weighed on platform scales and their weights were noted on their forearms. The total weight of a team of seven should not exceed 500 kilograms. On the day of the contest, the majority of them starved before the weigh in, and after the weigh in, ate as if there was no tomorrow.

Sunny chettayi and I went around, taking in the sights of the bustling churchyard.

Sasthamkunnil Kutty, the referee, was seven feet tall and weighed 145 kilograms. Dressed in a silk kurta and *mundu*, a *veshti* on his shoulder, half-shoe, and paan turning his mouth pillar-box red, Kutty was standing with the vicar in the rectory on the top floor of the church.

Occasional announcements were being made through the PA system about the contest. The teams huddled together at different parts of the yard, discussing their strategy. Seated amid a circle of nine young men beneath a tree, a karanavar was singing. The young men took up the chorus. Dressed in pink shorts and white tees, they were singing the Pannikkalippattu. When they sang about the incarnation of the boar with strength in its tusks to raise and hold whole worlds on them, I could see the strength flowing into their own sinews. The chorus of human voices accompanied by rhythmic claps was channelling the power of the whirlwind into them. Their tees bore the legend 'Karikkottakkary Devamata'.

Sunny chettayi and I stood where the tug rope was being readied. When he saw me clapping my hands in tandem with the song, he moved towards me and ribbed me, 'Kari . . . Kari . . . Karikkottakkary.'

The rope was laid out. The contest started with teams drawing lots. Kutty stood with his half-shoe placed on a rope that looked as thick as a decent-sized python. The teams of seven on either side of him ceremoniously touched the rope and then their foreheads to show their devoutness and invoke divine blessings. Kutty took up the hem of his mundu and tied it at half-mast. That was the first signal.

'Take up the rope,' the first order.

'Tighten the rope,' the second order.

Kutty tied the red ribbon that had been placed on the rope and positioned it over the centre line. He then blew the whistle. Would the ribbon pass the line on the left or the right? The cheering started. The drivers on either side twirled their *torthus* overhead and set the tempo for pulling and gave the signal for hanging. The first contest was won by Mundanoor St Joseph's team. The team who won the best of three moved to the next round.

Eventually, Karikkottakkary's turn came. Their opponent was the Kottukappara Sacred Heart team. Before the contest started, the man who had sung the song spat out the paan in a wide arc. He turned his back to his team and faced the spectators.

As soon as the 'tighten the rope' instruction rang out, he started to started to twirl the torthu above his head. And when the vocal syllables started and the whistle blew, in the blink of an eye the Karikkottakkary pullers did a smooth, surprising about-turn holding the rope on their shoulders. Heads down, they started to surge forward. The ribbon went far beyond the win line on their side. The karanavar was still singing.

As they won every test and, with the trophy of the bull buffalo in tow, went around the market, they were still singing the vocal syllables of the Pannikkalippattu song. The song got stuck in my mind from that day.

With a bowed head as I sat on the cement platform built around the lone fig tree that stood in the yard of the hall, I heard the rustle of a saree. I raised my eyes . . . it was my amma.

'Why did you come and sit here? Everyone's asking where's the boy who sang so well.'

I looked into her eyes. Unable to meet my eyes, which had already teared up before I heard her lie, she averted her gaze.

'Get up. People are at the feast. Sunny and Siby are busy serving guests. You go and join them.'

My helplessness deepened as I watched my mother dissemble.

'*Ammae . . .*'

She was defeated by my plaintive bleat. All the theatre in her demeanour and words collapsed. Placing her hand on my shoulder, she pleaded, 'Son, get up.'

Propped up by those words, I stood up. Her hand around my shoulder chased away my wretchedness. As the gloom lifted slowly, I had eyes only for her. I noticed how fair her cheeks were. Fair mother, fair father, fair relatives, and then my own dark arm. From that day, I started to doubt if I was an outsider in the Adhikarathil family that had made its mark in heaven and earth, its roots running deep into the rocks of antiquity and its proud crown spread in the sky of nobility. However, amma held me close to her.

Appan was supervising the service in the dining hall. My grandfather sat outside, exchanging pleasantries with everyone. Occasionally he would call out, 'Philippose.' It was a reminder to take care of those who mattered. My father split his time between minding the diners and attending to the guests outside. When my grandfather saw me, he gave me a quick stare. I felt afraid as if I had done something wrong. When I went in, my appan gave me a similar look. Unnerved by all those stares, I shrunk into a chair at the far side of the room.

Appan was striding the room with the vigour of one driving out a game on a hunt. Beef, pork and chicken went by, floating on platters. Everyone craved the pork. There was an unspoken secret behind it. The meat served was of wild boar. On the eastern border of the Adhikarathil family's lands were the Kodagu forests. The forests could be accessed through our estates.

Boar hunting was my appan's favourite pastime. Every year, at least four or five large black boars of the Kodagu forests fell to the unerring aim of my appan. The tharavad had five guns—two licensed and three unlicensed. My appan's favourite was the single-bore muzzleloader that Cheblan gunsmith of Idukki had fashioned for him. It had a flawlessly straight barrel made from an old Willys Jeep steering wheel, fixed on a stock made from wild jackwood.

Silvery gunpowder was available from the gun shop of zamindar Bopanna in Madikeri. The dry powder was poured into the barrel, and, with coconut husk and a ramrod, the charge was tamped in place. A metal round and a few glass pieces made up the projectile. Confident of his marksmanship, appan always used steel ball bearings as projectiles. Most of the people eschewed the use of lead projectiles since, if they missed the prey and hit a rock, the lead may ricochet back at them.

The guns and charges were kept in the bungalow inside the estate. On hunt nights, my Johnny *pappan* too would be in the party. He always carried the double-barrel muzzleloader. On his shoulder would be a bag that contained salt, chilli powder, turmeric powder, two rudraksha-handle daggers, a skewer, a chopper, two small aluminium vessels, a roll of twine, projectiles and the gun powder pouch; in his hand a five-cell Eveready flashlight.

After their return, appan would narrate every moment of the hunt to none of us in particular. Therefore, each of their hunts was embedded in my mind. The route taken by the boars was easily distinguishable from the rooting around they did with their snouts and tusks. Once the spoor was identified, a comfortable spot was chosen downwind, from where a clean shot was possible. It had to be cleared and leaves and branches spread on the ground for cushioning. And then the wait started. It could be hours; hours of suspense, tedium and discomfort. Even moving the numb legs and hands had to be done ever so silently.

The slightest movement was enough for the wary boars to avoid their usual path. Leeches, fleas and centipedes could bite for all they were worth, but the hunters would not stir.

Eventually, enveloped in darkness, the sounder of boars would arrive nosing the ground along their beaten path. Appan's ears would catch the first sounds of their impending arrival. The distant snorting of the leader, the rustle of leaves underfoot . . . the barrel of the gun would be kept pointed at the path.

The torch was never brought out for boar hunting. Smaller animals, barking deer, the giant squirrel are all attracted to light and once they are caught in the beam, they freeze. It is easy thereafter—aim at the middle of the glowing eyes, shoot, and they will fall. Boars alone cannot be pinned down using the spear of light.

They can sense the danger posed by the light of even a wayward firefly. My father knew that it was literally a shot in the dark. Depending on the size of the boar, the ear is about eighteen inches from the tip of the snout. The shot should be aimed at the spot behind the ear. Even if it misses the brain, it should hit the heart through the neck. The animal will not fall if the round hits any further back. With the searing round inside it, the boar will keep running. After weeks or even months of suffering, it will fall prey to the fox or vultures. Appan always killed them with headshots; his shots never went beyond the head.

The first person to reach the fallen boar would be Johnny pappan. The skewer, sharper than a dagger, would be driven up from under the jaw into the brain. The little life that was left in the boar would leave it, and it would turn into pork.

The carcass would be dragged to the plain ground and gutted. Salt and turmeric would be applied on the flesh. A carrying pole would be fashioned out of a sturdy branch, the boar's body tied to it and carried on shoulders down the valley. One of the shoulder pieces appan would bring home. The rest was divided between relatives after cutting it up in the estate.

The dining room now looked like the yard from where the pork cuts had been taken away by the people. Only the family heads of the Adhikarathil family were left. The family reunion was evaluated under the auspices of my grandfather. The consensus was that this was the best so far. When the assembly was dispersing, Outhakutty uncle, who had come from Peravoor, passed a comment, 'Philippose, your son's song and all that were good. However, it wasn't something that behoved our family. It felt as if a Pulaya family had conducted a feast.'

When we were driving back in the jeep, appan and my grandfather seated in front looked grim.

Chapter 2

Vimalagiri College

The Adhikarathil mansion is about 2 kilometres to the east of Malom town. At the time my great-grandfather, Kuncheriya, arrived here, Malom was still part of the forest. Only tribals lived there. Unlike other immigrants, who would come with all their worldly possessions bundled up and dependents in tow, he did not queue up in front of the landowner's caretaker's house, begging for land. With two valets in tow, he arrived at Kanhangad by train and took a room in a lodge. The next day he arrived at the landowner Nayanar's house on a bullock cart. Seated on a chair, he spoke as an equal of the landowner. A landowner from Thiruvithamkoor was conducting business with one from Malabar. As a token of the Adhikarathil family's respects and gratification, five bundles of Jaffna tobacco and one bottle of Scotch whisky were given to Nayanar.

My great-granddad Kuncheriya made it clear that he was not seeking ten or twelve acres like the other desperate arrivals, and that he needed five hills to start plantations. Once he had a look at the offered land and was satisfied, ready payment would be made, and the deed registered.

My great-granddad went with the caretaker to assess the hills. When they reached the spot where the Adhikarathil mansion stands now, he paused. He looked up at the sky and let his sixth sense take over. The wind direction and sun were favourable. Almost four acres of plain ground without inclines and precipices. A rivulet flowed from north to south as a plentiful source of water. He stood for a while with his eyes closed, his mind busy with calculations. He asked for a chopper from the workers and cut a straight branch from the gnarled devil's tree and drove it into the land after checking the directions and lie of the land. After completing the document work, before leaving, great-granddad had a house built there with bamboo rafters, lemongrass thatch and bamboo mat walls.

On his second coming, he had an entourage of workers and labourers in tow. Paniyas, Karimpalas—tribes of aboriginals— boars and other animals were flushed out by the game drive system and put to flight. The dark men who did not run away were made to join the gang of workers and used in hunting boars and other animals which were apportioned and eaten.

Then started the felling of the trees. The Muslim traders were the timber buyers. If other migrants had to fell trees, they had to take permission from the landowner or his caretaker and pay a toll. The Adhikarathil family members could fell the trees as they wished. The landowner never demurred.

The mahogany, Burma ironwood, hopea and cadama trees felled in the upper reaches had to be reached to Chaitra Vahini River. After they cut down the massive trees with a girth that matched the dimension of a water well, debarked, trimmed the sapwood and cut a tow-hole in their heartwood, the loggers would withdraw.

Next on the scene were the elephants and the pullers. Taking the coir hawsers that were tied to the tow-hole between their teeth, elephants would drag the trees. Like mini trains running through the forest and flattening the undergrowth, the trees moved on. The furrowed ruts created by the elephants in those days are the roads of the present-day Malom.

Even as the lumber was coming down the slopes, in the Thachoth fields of Malom, brick kilns started to sprout—a novel sight for the denizen of Malom. Walls started to go up, laid with the bright red fired bricks. The elephants tugged and placed mature, right-sized trees for the saw-wielders. By the time the woodwork was over and the truss for the roof mounted, roof tiles arrived from Basil Mission's factory in Mangalore. It was Malom's first house with a tiled roof— the European-style Adhikarathil bungalow with rooms, chambers and corridors.

Mathai, the oldest son of great-granddad Kuncheriya, went to Iritty to start plantation estates. My grandfather Kunjepp inherited the tharavad. Before Kuncheriya died, a few concrete-roofed houses had come up around Kanhangad. Kunjepp asked his father's opinion on remodelling our house and having a concrete roof for the front portion. His answer was to narrate the story of the nouveau riche Kallumaakkal Devasyachan.

Leaving behind his wretched days in a grass-roofed hut, Devasyachan made a bagful of money by brokering some big deals in Ernakulam. One of the reputed families in Ernakulam suggested an alliance between him and their daughter. He decided that by the time they came for the traditional pre-wedding visit, the roof of his house should be tiled. Everyone thought that he would buy new tiles. But he bought old tiles from a Thalassery Muslim at triple the going price. By using the blackened and mossy tiles, his tharavad was transformed into one with a long-standing heredity.

'Kunjepp, the Adhikarathil family doesn't have the need to buy heredity and antiquity by paying money. Fashion and fads will come and go. The nobility of one's heredity alone stays undiminished. Even after a century, there will not be a house in all of Malom that shall have the prestige of the house I have built.'

As years passed, my grandfather and my father realized the truth in those words. The huge courtyard in front of the house lay in the shade of the watery rose apple, mango and jackfruit trees. A nine-foot-wide veranda ran along three sides of the house with eighteen single wooden pillars holding up the roof truss. Brass strips bound the top and bottom of the pillars. A carved door opened into the centre courtyard from the veranda. All the front windows had carved panels. From the centre courtyard corridors led to the kitchen and rooms.

At the end of one of the corridors was a stairwell. The first floor had many rooms with wooden ceilings. During Maundy Thursday and Christmas, all the rooms would be full of people. As long as my great-grandfather and great-grandmother were alive, the Passover Bread and Christmas cake cutting was done in the tharavad. Johnny pappan and

his family, my aunts and their husbands and children all
would be present. They would bring gifts for the elders.

Maundy Thursday was the more important occasion for
the family. From the time Uncle Kuttappan became blind,
I used to read the 'Puthen Pana', the Malayalam poem on
the life of Jesus Christ written by the German Jesuit priest
popularly known as Arnos Pathiri.

> *The day before the Unleavened Bread*
> *Was to be eaten, asked the disciples,*
> *'Where shall we arrange for you*
> *To eat the Passover Bread?'*
> *Lord of the lords, the Messiah*
> *Spoke to the apostles . . .*

Everyone remained in the centre courtyard listening to
my recitation of the 'Puthen Pana'. After the morning
mass, women got busy preparing the Passover Bread. Oil
was applied on garlic which was then kept in the sun in
the courtyard. The dried garlic could be skinned easily by
rolling them between the palms. Soaked split black-eyed
beans, garlic, cumin seeds, grated coconut, and rice powder
were mixed and kneaded to make the dough.

After making the sign of the cross and benediction, my
grandfather would prepare the dough and, when it was soft
enough, push the platter towards the womenfolk; they had
to take on from there. The dough was placed on an oblong
strip of plantain leaf and the four corners folded in. The
wedge-shaped bread was stacked in a large copper vessel
and steamed. At the bottom of the vessel, coconut leaves
with their spine removed were kept, wound into a circle,

the centre of which would be filled with coconut husk. The water level would be maintained below the coconut husk layers.

This bread was called Inri appam—taking off from the abbreviation INRI in Christian motifs which stood for *Iesus Nazarenus, Rex Iudaeorum*, meaning Jesus of Nazareth, the King of the Jews. The Passover Bread would be made on a tin-coated bronze platter. After pouring the dough into the platter, my grandfather would recite a silent prayer. He would take strips from the tender coconut leaves received by him on Palm Sunday and make a crucifix on the top of the bread. Amid the recitation of prayers, the Passover Bread would be placed in the middle of the stacked Inri appams. The edges of the vessel would be lined with a cloth, the lid placed on it and the edges sealed with rice-powder dough.

The bread would be steamed at high pressure simulating how the Messiah's heart was scorched before his scourge started. The vessel had to be taken off the fire at the precise moment—if the bread was scorched or was found cracked, it presaged a calamity that was to befall the family.

By 5 p.m., the vessel would be opened. Before the milk was boiled at night, the children would start consuming the Inri appam. The Passover Milk was made by boiling coconut milk infused with jaggery, cardamom, dry ginger and tender coconut leaves.

At the time of cutting the Passover Bread, every family member had to be in attendance. My grandad used to do the honours. The bread, cut into square slices, would be distributed along with the Passover Milk and poovan banana, depending on the age and size of the recipient.

The reading of the 'Pana' followed. Everyone spent the night in the tharavad. They dispersed only after attending the Good Friday service at the church.

After the family reunion, when everyone dispersed, I felt as if it was a Good Friday. After a change of clothes, when I emerged into the centre courtyard, my father and grandfather were lying there in wait for me. My father was the first to speak.

'You are my only son . . . the scion of Adhikarathil Philippose. You have no paths of your own. The only path to tread on is that of the family . . . If anyone else strays from his path, no one will notice it. But you . . . if you as much as turn your head, everyone will know of it. That is your fate.'

My grandfather butted in. 'Philippose, you don't have to beat around the bush.' He turned towards me. 'You should live not like a Pulaya, but as a Christian. A Syrian Christian with centuries-old tradition. A Christian from the Adhikarathil fold that has in its lineage beatified saints. Hereafter, you shall do nothing that will cause comments or set people talking. Do you understand? Now scram!'

Even as I was being dismissed from his presence, I could see my mother inside with her head bowed. I could not stay there anymore. Carrying my torthu and soap I went to the stream.

A tributary of Chaitra Vahini flowed through our estate. We bathed and washed clothes in that stream full of smooth, rounded granite stones. For a long time, I lay submerged in one of its summertime trenches.

What was the fate that my father was talking of? My dark skin is that fate. My blackness that I viewed only when

I looked in the mirror had started to stare at me from every direction. My fate. Am I the cause of my fate?

If at least my father could have realized this, I wished.

A howling wind from the west carried a gusty rain within it which it refused to let loose. The sky was filled with smoky, swirling clouds. Thin lightning sped across like a golden thread releasing a spinning top. The black clouds descended on the hills. Grazing the tops of the rubber estate, the sky caressed the arjun trees by the side of the stream. It started to rain, setting off tiny explosions of watery crowns on the surface of the stream.

Raindrops got caught in my eyelashes. Wiping them off, when I looked, the long lashes of rain were sweeping the paths and raising fine dust. The rain was now coming down at full pelt—on the dried meadows; on the boulders crawling with molluscs; on the dust bowls; on the washing stones with licks of soap pasted on them.

My secondary school examination results came out after two weeks. I had scored only three hundred and seven marks out of six hundred, not enough to get me admission under the merit quota in the prestigious Vimalagiri College run by the Thalassery Diocese. Notwithstanding that, my name was on the first list of admissions.

The vast rocky yard of the college had grass sprouts resembling green dust sprinkled by the breeze.

'Shall I drop you in the car?' my father had asked me. I preferred to take the bus. Stepping on to the damp grass sprouts on the path, I started my life in the college like other students, without the pomp and show of the Adhikarathil family.

Huddled in small groups, the freshmen shared and dispelled their anxieties. Jojy Jacob, who hailed from Cherupuzha, was boasting about how his admission had been wangled. His paternal uncle was a member of the Pastoral Council of the Diocese. His uncle had met the right people in person and that was how he had come fifth in the management quota list. He made sure everyone knew of the connection that his family had with the bishop. I thought of my own father. I was the first name on the management quota list.

On the third day of college, I was standing on the first floor, gazing at the sprawling rocky terrain of the campus. It was raining. A dark-skinned boy like me was running towards the college from the urinals which were some distance away from the main building. Pulling up his trouser legs with one hand, and with the other above his head to protect it from the raindrops, he was zigzagging between the others holding umbrellas. I had seen him the day before also, running similarly.

He came up, shaking his head vigorously to get rid of the rainwater and wiping his hands dry. In those three days, I had not got acquainted with him. Let alone me, no one else in the class had befriended him. When I thought of it, I realized no one had made friends with me either. We were the only two who had made no friends.

I kept gazing at him steadily as he shook his head, irritated by the dampness, and tried to wipe the water off with a handkerchief. Eventually, I caught his eye. His eyes had a kind of defiant servility that he could not hide despite his best intentions. His provenance was stamped on his face, which still had raindrops streaming down.

'You're from Karikkottakkary, aren't you?' I asked without any preamble or premeditation.

'Yes,' he replied, pleased. 'Do you know anyone there?'

'I'd come there last year to watch the tug-of-war.'

'We were all there, singing songs during the tug-of-war.' His face brightened. His friendship could have sprouted its tender leaves because it was watered by the raindrops of the Pannikkalippattu. My first friend in Vimalagiri College—Sebastian V.D. from Karikkottakkary.

One day, Seban asked me, 'Aren't you OEC?' I did not know then what OEC was, which later I understood stood for Other Eligible Castes, which encompassed people from the Scheduled Castes who had converted to Christianity.

'Aren't you a Christian convert?' he expanded on the question.

'No.'

'Well, I have told everyone that neither am I, but when they hear of Karikkottakkary, they all know I am a newly minted Christian.'

That night, I was not thinking about his sense of inferiority as a new Christian. I was thinking about his complexion, puffy cheeks and salmon-coloured, thick, flaccid lips. He had decided I was also a newly converted Christian.

For the first time in my life, I cried over my complexion, my physique and my name.

My Lord, why, instead of casting me in the same exquisite mould of the Adhikarathil family, have you set me apart?

With my tear-dimmed eyes, when I looked at the indistinct form in the mirror, I saw Sebastian there. I found him abhorrent. For some days after that, I stopped talking to him. Unaware of my animus, time and again he tried to make conversation with me. I kept avoiding him.

All the college lecturers were fair-skinned, believers of the Church. The general opinion was that Father Leo Alakkal—author of a long poem on the sainted Sister Alphonsa—being its principal was a matter of great pride for the college. Father Alakkal was my father's friend. Nevertheless, he behaved as if he did not know me from Adam. Although I also ignored him, whenever I thought of Soumya C. Chacko, his niece, his shadow would rise before me like a boulder in the stream.

Soumya C. Chacko was a resident of the hostel run by the Sisters of the Holy Wounds adjacent to their convent. I felt that she was the right height for me. I started to notice her more after this thought entered my mind.

As she walked along the gravel-strewn path from the hostel to the college, many a time I stood sucking in my breath at the sight of her smooth, rounded, shapely calves being caressed by the stalks of grass. The vigilant eyes of Father Alakkal protected his sister's daughter like armour. However, his piercing stares were not deterrent enough to veer me from my path of love.

For her sake, I started to tuck my shirt into my trousers and wear a belt. I applied the face cream I had procured from Kanhangad and topped it with talcum powder. I darkened my sparse moustache, colouring the gaps with kohl. I applied fragrant hair oil none in the college could obtain and combed my hair in every way and style.

In eight months, she smiled eleven times at me. I spent the intervals between those smiles in reverie—dreaming about trips we would take defying Father Alakkal. We laughed at tricking the rainbow-coloured carps and minnows in Chaitra Vahini River to kiss my dark feet placed by her pink fingers as counterpoint. As we walked along the leaf-strewn paths of the Adhikarathil estates, frightened by the serpent that rose from among the gin berry bushes, she embraced me.

As far as I was concerned, she attended the classes for my sake. During intervals, sitting amid her friends, she sang 'Guardian Angel from Heaven So Bright' with a slight lisp for me. During Malayalam classes, when Lukas sir taught us the poem 'Remember Sometimes' she turned her fair and comely face towards the right side and remained with her eyes shut also for me.

She spoke to me for the first time on the sixth day of the ninth month after we had met. On her usual route, as I stood beneath the whistling pine tree, picking apart the needle-like leaves at their nodes and stacking them up in my hand, she smiled at me. And squinting her wide eyes she asked, 'Eranimos, you come from Karikkottakkary, don't you?'

'No.' Though I had spoken, since she had gone past me, she did not hear me. She was giving more attention to a friend who was with her.

I did not weep that night. I recalled that the twelve smiles Soumya C. Chacko had directed at me in those nine months were all the same. I was crushed by the realization that all of them were swinging towards the question that she had asked me.

The shattered mirror of love reminded me of Seban. In my college, I was someone else; I was not the scion of the Adhikarathil family. My ire at Seban was unwarranted. What he thought of me was the reality.

Soumya C. Chacko merely underscored that reality. The talcum powder that I patted on to my face was not the reality; my black skin was. On the same night, I wiped off all the pictures that romance had painted on my body during those eight lovesick months.

The next day I spoke to Seban.

'I had known that you are not from Karikkottakkary and are a member of the most reputable family of Malom. I had asked that question for a lark.' He consoled me by embracing his own racial loneliness to himself. I placed my hands on his supple, hairless forearms and looked into his eyes. I must have seen in them the moistness of a deep-rooted feeling of inferiority, which, at my age then, I could not have fully comprehended.

He took my hand and stroked the back of my palm. That was a first for me. It was a rain-bearing breeze that helped seeds of friendship sprout in a bleak, rocky field of alienation. He was caressing carefully the fine hair on my own forearm. He was enjoying touching the sprinkling of a felicitous growth that he himself was deprived of. Our clasped hands were the promise of a long-enduring and strong heritage. In my life, in the years that followed, Sebastian V.D. the hair-loving, newly minted Christian youth, became my dearest friend.

Chapter 3

Sultan Cave

I wore full trousers for the first time when I started my eighth class. My father took me to Kanhangad, bought a coffee-coloured fabric and got it stitched from a local tailor. As I roamed the valleys of Malom clad in those drain-pipe trousers, the people looked at me in wonderment. Even when I moved to Vimalagiri College, trousers had not become common in Malom.

Much before we in the valley had started to wear trousers, it was common-wear in Karikkottakkary. When I was there for the tug-of-war event, I did not check out the people from Karikkottakkary singularly; there were people from everywhere for that event. I noticed their clothes only when I accompanied Seban to Karikkottakkary.

I saw a man digging a pit to plant elephant yam, dressed in a safari suit. A man in a rich-looking jacket and lungi was sitting and chewing paan in front of a kiosk built with coconut thatch. Most of the people wore ill-fitting trousers.

The denizens of Karikkottakkary lived as if in some village in the West, dressed in gowns, jackets and trousers.

Karikkottakkary town grew in the shadow of the rustic crucifix of the Devamata Latin Church. The church stood on an island of black laterite. Where the laterite was submerged by sand, Nambiar mango—a speciality cultivar of the Kuttiattoor region—njaval and ilanji trees prospered. They all needed the scorching heat of the summers. They remained listless during the rains; invigorated during summers, they bloomed and flourished.

Below the church was the paved road along which stood three or four old buildings, two of which were double-storeyed. One belonged to the church; one of its rooms housed the Mission League office, the other, the Devamata Music Band. Across the buildings were the grocery shop run by Kunjikka, Antony Tailors, Kalakki Bhaskaran's barber shop, the local agriculture office, Maruthapuram Jose's teashop . . . with its old buildings, gravelly paths and Nambiar mango trees, the town lay like a hoary cloth that was spread on one corner of the globe.

As I walked in the company of Seban, people dressed in Western attire looked suspiciously at me, a stranger in their midst. They looked like characters out of comic books. Turning the quiet scene into a terrifying one, two apparitions showed in front of us—dressed in cut-away trousers, jackets and hats; two blind men. One of them held a white stick which had a bicycle bell screwed on. The other held a wooden bucket.

A skinned, bleeding buffalo head, with a protruding row of teeth, bulbous eyes and minatory horns, stuck out of the bucket. Bones still sticky with blood and offal were stuck densely around the buffalo's head like a halo. Muttering to the bucket-holder, the man with the stick led him, ringing the bell often. As I stood gaping at the zombies, Seban said, 'Children of Father Nickolaus . . . that's food for the pigs in that bucket.'

We were on our study holiday before our first-year examination. My father was unaware of this visit to Karikkottakkary. The grass stalks had withered and collapsed in the heat of the day. In some places, they had caught fire and were scorched black in patches, resembling maps of land and sea.

The laterite quarries which had begun to pockmark other parts of the valley had not yet come into Karikkottakkary; its laterite was too hard to be hacked manually with axes and cut into bricks.

Seban's house was on a plateau atop a small rise. The yard around it seemed to have readied itself to receive the summer rains. In between the rocky protrusions that looked like carapaces, was the soft black soil. New ridges had been shored up around which saplings and seedlings were planted—hemispheres for tapioca, flatter ellipses for yam and elephant yam, square patches for ginger, trapezoid ones for sweet potato, circles around ironwood irrigation conduits made for the greater and lesser yam . . . in his agricultural pursuits, Seban's father, Vedikunju, had made the land a celebration of geometric patterns.

Kunjettan, resting on the polished cow-dung floor, welcomed me while humming a song. There was only a thin, basket-shaped metal-frame chair with woven plastic braids on that stoop. I chose to follow Seban into the house. The carbon-black mixed cow dung floor inside was smooth and polished like a black mirror. The clay walls were made shiny with the resin of the bay tree. They had tiled the roof the previous year using ironwood rafters and bamboo crosspieces. The entire house looked remarkably compact and had an excellent finish. In a clay-lined recess in the wall stood an idol of Our Lady of Velankanni.

'Before he lost his fingers, *achchachan* had carved it on a soapstone using his pen knife,' Seban said.

Kunjettan lifted his hand—only stubs remained of his thumb, ring and little fingers.

'In the fireworks for the church feast, my fingers were given as offerings for Mother Mary. Although I have stopped doing fireworks, people still call me Vedikunju,' Kunjettan laughed as he said it. His nickname came from *vedi*, short for *vedikettu,* or fireworks, in the vernacular.

Seban's mother had heard of the Adhikarathil family. Theyyamma *chechi* was making arrangements to welcome her son's famous friend.

I found the boiled dried tapioca and beef tripe delicious. Every house in Karikkottakkary stored dried tapioca. Along the valley, during the tapioca season, everyone dried tapioca as insurance against starvation; however, in Karikkottakkary it was a ritual. They called it Kappavattu Kalyanam, the Dry Tapioca Wedding.

In order to escape the scorching sun, the preparations were done during nights. Tapioca grown in everyone's plots was collected and piled up; soil and skin were removed by women and children; men sliced the bleached-look tubers into thin slices.

Some of the tapioca-slicers were good raconteurs. They would tell stories the whole night as the slicing went on.

Stories that happened and did not happen in places that existed and were imaginary. But every story would be narrated with verisimilitude as if they had been eyewitnesses. Some others were singers. Their old songs would keep up the tempo of skinning and slicing.

Plucked chicken and big slices of buffalo meat would be roasted in the embers in the peripheries of the huge fire pits on which the tapioca was boiled. Before they were taken out, men would gulp down moonshine. The relatives who came as guests would get the lion's share.

The semi-cooked tapioca slices were taken out and spread on the black laterite to be sun-dried. It took three days of sunshine to desiccate the tapioca completely. Once they were gathered and tied up in gunny bags, the householders let out a sigh of relief. Until they ran out of these stocks, starvation would be kept at bay.

In Karikkottakkary, these efforts, spread over days and nights, were no drudgery; they were a celebration, a festival . . . filled with folk tales, songs, arrack, grilled chicken and visiting relatives. The people of Karikkottakkary ensured that every year the Kappavattu Kalyanam was a memorable one.

Dried tapioca was a staple food round the year in Seban's house. It was kept soaked in water overnight and boiled in water the next morning. Without mashing it, grated coconut, chillies and turmeric were added. Theyyamma chechi kept the boiled tapioca in front of me with great reluctance. Buffalo entrails were used to make the tripe dish.

In our family too, dishes were made with tripe. One of our workers used to fetch it without anyone else knowing about it, wash and cut it, and give it to us. The entrails had a distinct dungy smell. They were like a patchwork quilt—in some places they had brown checks; in others they resembled fleece; some portions were like honeycombs. The omasum, or bible, was a spherical portion which, when torn out, was like a book with many pages, each of which had to be flipped over, scraped and cleaned. After soaking it in hot water, if it was scraped with a knife, the outer layer would be removed, revealing a white sheet. Since preparing and eating tripe was infra dig, no one outside the Adhikarathil family was ever aware that we consumed it.

The tripe in Seban's house tasted different. It had been roasted crisp over slow heat in a cast iron wok along with curry leaves, spices, ginger and pepper, interspersed by white coconut slices, elevating the visual appeal. As she watched us wolf down the tripe, Seban's sister, Bindu, exclaimed a repulsed, 'Aiyyae.' She was not fond of tripe.

After the meal, everyone got out into the yard. I sat on a rock in the shade of the ironwood tree as a spectator. A student of seventh standard, Bindu was wearing a blue gown and cap. Though a Western dress, it suited her.

It was the first time I witnessed how manual work could become an art. In Adhikarathil lands, what I used to witness was the tedium of workers doing things mechanically. Commands issued by my appan used to whirl around in that place. Here, in Seban's place, the breeze of affection was blowing gently.

Work went on amid laughter and the workers ribbing one another. Kunjettan assessed the maturity of yams and cut up the mature ones. The leaves were kept aside for making curry. Colocasia and ginger tubers were dug and shaken free of the soil and cleaned up. Turmeric piles grew, taking on a golden glow. Snipping off the adventitious fibrous roots, tapioca tubers were pulled out. Those from which fungus has to be removed were selected and stacked separately.

Theyyamma chechi prepared cow dung solution in a big wooden vat. The selected bulbs, saplings and seedlings were dipped in it and kept in the shade for drying. Sebastian and Bindu fetched dried cattle dung powder in a bamboo basket and dried leaves in a thatched basket and stacked them beside the ridges. Their dog, Sahai, was frolicking in the fine dust of the ginger patches. Hens had a hearty meal of maggots they unearthed by scratching around in the cattle dung powder. Sometime in between all this, Kunjettan broke into a song:

Alas and alack, our good neighbours,
Our house has been burgled.

Seban, Bindu and Theyyamma chechi joined in the chorus.

One is a darkie, one is a whitey,
Another is stout and strong;
One took a banana bunch, the other
A coconut bunch, and the third
Stole one and a half rupees;
On the way they fled a papaya plant was uprooted,
Pappadams were spread and dung pits filled . . .
Alas and alack, our good neighbours,
Our house has been burgled . . .

The dog, the hens, the crow perched on the ironwood branch, the cow resting under the mango tree all swayed to the tune of the song.

Later, Seban told me, 'The rains come when achchachan sings. Within three days of him getting the saplings and bulbs ready, the rains arrive.'

On that day, by the time I reached home, it had started to rain.

After the summer rains, by the time the monsoons arrived, all the land in Karikkottakkary would have turned green; different hues of verdure—golden green, blue-green, dark green, pastel green . . .

Our family lands in Malom, too, had a cornucopia of crops. However, they lacked the orderliness and hallowed look of Karikkottakkary. My grandfather used to say, 'Adhikarathil wealth is not the crops; it is the land. When it rains, we till and sow not for the family but for the workers to provide for their families.'

No other farmer in Malom received the kind of harvest that the Adhikarathil family received for the cultivation that they did for the sake of workers in their thirteen and three-fourth acres.

Johnny pappan would arrive on the day of the first rain, just as springs would start gushing out of the ground. They hunt fish on that day, an annual event. In the euphoria of having mated, the river fish swim upstream to spawn in the Chaitra Vahini River. In the heat of their fiery libidinous instinct to forge the links of their generations, nothing can impede them.

Leaping over the torrents, their floodplain breeding run proceeds. As the fish get attracted by the light that moves along the banks of the stream, their leaping surface-breaks end with them dying on the sharp edge of the sword. The snake-like Malabar spiny-eel; the olive barb fish that resembles the jackfruit leaf; the cylindrical Curmuca barb; the orange chromide which is the pearlspot fish of the fresh water; sucker fish; the frogs that leap at the light of the flambeaus—everything landed in my appan's sack.

From the sack emptied on the floor of the mission house, the fish would tumble out in heaps . . .

Martyrs to their own rudely interrupted passion.

On the night of the fish hunt, my appan and Johnny pappan would eat only frog meat, roasted with only salt, pepper and turmeric. The moment it was cooked, the meat would bloat up and get separated from the bone.

'Eranimos, come have a couple of frog legs to avoid getting asthma,' my father would invite me.

That year, as he took out a pair of scorched rear legs of a frog and handed them over to me, appan asked me, 'Why did you go to Karikkottakkary?'

By the time I replied, 'To borrow a book from my classmate,' and started to bite into the frog leg, my father's heavy hand landed on my back.

'You need no truck with the Pulayas of that place. You son-of-a-whore, you'll only do things that you are told not to do, won't you?'

Johnny pappan, till then sitting as if he was mulling over a humiliating secret, grabbed and took appan off me. My father had not finished.

'I told you long ago that you are a member of the Adhikarathil family. There are people you can associate with. And there are those you can't. If you don't keep that in mind and behave, I'll finish you.'

Beneath the teapoy that bore the frog meat were a bottle of cashew arrack and a glass.

'Let go, Pylee, from now on he'll keep appropriate company.' My uncle tried to cool things down.

I turned on my heel and walked into the kitchen. I flung the frog leg in my hand out into the rain. My mother was marinating fish pieces that had been washed in starch water with raw mustard and turmeric paste. She was weeping silently. I looked at her and said, 'I'll go again to Karikkottakkary.'

Her sobs became more pronounced.

I returned to Karikkottakkary before the rainy season ended. My father was on a trip to Ramapuram.

Karikkottakkary in the rains is a different sight altogether. The black laterite of the summer disappears. The sprouts of mission grass cover the laterite and hold conversations with the breeze. The seeds and saplings that had become one with the soil hold a show with their fronds, branches and tendrils, and flourish. Now bereft of fruits, the foliage of the Nambiar mango trees turn dark. Blackened by rain, only a few cashew nuts hide in the trees.

There was no rain on that day. Seban's family was out in their plot of land—weeding at the root of the tapioca plants, tying vines to the support trees, shoring up the soil around the yam and ginger plants. By afternoon, the land had its tidy look back.

When we sat down for lunch, Theyyamma chechi said sadly, 'There's no curry.'

Yet there was an assortment of minor fishes in gravy, sautéed long beans leaves, and sour mango pickle. Bindu served herself tiny quantities of everything and started to eat.

'Stop putting on airs. From now on you have to eat your fill, lass.' When Theyyamma chechi scolded her, I noticed something. The rains had brought some changes in her too.

When we were lazing around in the afternoon, Seban asked me, 'Have you seen a cave?'

'No.'

'We have a large one here. Sultan Cave.'

'Shall we go and see?' I was very keen.

Bindu wanted to accompany us. Seban stopped her.

Sultan Hill stood like a tower of Karikkottakkary to its east, as if it had leapt up using the rear leg for leverage. A hill clothed in lemongrass; if one was not careful, their razor edges would slash the skin. Thousands of flexible swords, *urumi*s, that swayed in the breeze—the sentinels of Sultan. Keeping the flashing blades away from us with sticks, we climbed the hill. When we reached the top, it felt like being atop a galloping horse. The strong wind seemed to be blowing from centuries back. Below us lay swaying lands to be overrun in our military campaigns.

'Long live Tipu Sultan,' shouted Seban, for no reason.

We found a small pond in the middle of a large rock. We washed our faces in the water. As he drank the water, Seban said, 'This never dries up, not even in the summer.'

'Do you want to see the Womb? Come, let me show you.'

He suddenly grabbed my hand and started to run. We ran up to the edge of a crevice in the middle of two huge rocks. It took me many years to appreciate the sense of humour of the person who would have called it the Womb for the first time. Yet, somehow, my heart told me the womb would look the same.

Seban went to one edge of the Womb and keeping his hands on either half looked down into the crevice. It was dark inside—the pitch darkness of a womb. I also knelt and looked down.

My feet slipped without any warning.

The sound of Seban shouting '*Edaaa . . .*' came from overhead as I was descending.

There was a bellow from the darkness. 'Who the fuck are you?' Shivering with fright, my body came in contact with another human being. There was someone else in the Womb other than me. I found myself lying on soft ground. Up above me was a slice of sky in parenthesis. Seban was screaming at the top of his lungs.

'Shut the fuck up.'

From inside the Womb, a strong hand clamped on my arm.

'To see whose fucking cunt did you crawl in here?'

The shouting brought me close to tears.

'Don't moan, there are steps cut out on the rock face. Climb up.'

He pushed me up. I used the footholds as handholds to haul myself up. A man appeared behind me resembling a broad patch of black laterite, with black grass-like hair all over him.

'Oh, it was you, Yonachan?' Seban looked surprised.

'Who is this runt?' he gestured towards me.

'He's my friend. His house is in Malom.'

'And in Malom, what's his family's name?' he turned and looked as he started to leave.

'Adhikarathil.'

'Whose son, in that family?'

'Philippose.'

When I uttered that, he stared at me. He suddenly became deflated; his brashness oozed out. From that hollowed-out man words out came like a whisper, 'Why did you come here?'

His head dropped; eventually, the breeze seemed to carry him downhill; he looked so lost.

Seban asked me, 'Do you know him from before?'

'Who's he?

'Mankuruni Yonachan. He makes hooch, and therefore that name. His expression changed when he heard your family name. Ah, let it be. Anyway, one thing I have understood. He is "still" is inside the Womb.' Seban was laughing.

Who is he? Who *is* he? My mind kept bothering me.

Seban was careful not to let me fall again. I washed myself in the pond and got rid of all the mud and soil. A strong breeze was blowing from the west; it bore the smell of rain.

'Let's go to the cave.'

As we walked down, carefully parting the lemongrass, rain arrived. I saw the opening of the cave through the gauzy veil of rain. A small square opening, carvings around which were crumbling. The only adornment were the ferns and climbers that were growing on the laterite. Roots could be seen snaking through the wall of the cave and diving into the earth. Holding my damp hand, Seban walked to the cave opening. He threw stones into the cave to make sure no wild animals were lurking inside. He crawled inside through the opening. It was very dark inside.

'Come in,' his voice echoed inside.

It was strangely warm inside. I could see Seban after my eyes adjusted to the darkness. The cave was larger than I had imagined; it could house a meeting of around thirty people. The walls were, by far, dry; seepage could be seen in a few places. The popular belief was that the cave had been made at the time of Tipu Sultan's Malabar campaigns.

Seban took off his shirt. His wet body gleamed like a serpent's back.

'Take off your shirt and wring it,' he said as he wiped his head.

When I was taking off my shirt, Seban moved close to me. His odour reminded me of petrichor.

'Towel your head,' he offered me the torthu.

As I started to do so, he moved to my rear.

'I'll do something for you.'

The earthy scent enveloped me from behind. His serpentine body had moulted completely.

As my armours were taken off one by one, he nipped me on my neck. My flared nostrils tried to drink in the smell of his brand of petrichor. What I smelled was not his odour but that of an ur-man. The scent of humanity. His hands started to knead the earth around my waist. The sweat drops on my chest he mixed with the earth. He was priming me.

I swam with the tides in waters under which I throbbed; crawled over the petrichor-emissions of the earth like a serpent; tasted the salinity, sourness, astringency of fruits, berries and raw flesh. I went under like a seed, churning over the black soil of the land. I sprouted, grew leaves and branches and soared into the skies. From the heavens, I looked down at the earth. Where was I floating to?

'Seban, stop!'

'This is just the beginning.' He did not stop.

This is death. End of the world. Shaking off my corporeal state, I transmigrated into a free soul. There was no Seban; no cave; no world; it was just me and my soul, a will-o'-the-wisp.

'Seban, I am dying . . .'

'Sweetheart, no, you are coming . . .'

The world ended . . . the will-o'-the-wisp vanished . . . darkness . . . only darkness remained. I dropped like a dry leaf. Catching the droplets from the falling leaf in his palm, Seban laughed.

'It's pretty dilute . . .'

I collapsed on to the torthu that Seban spread on the ground. With his soft hands, he rubbed the clear cum on the inside of my thighs. I lay with my eyes closed. I was being smothered by the earth. In the languor that followed my return from the verge of death, I gripped his shoulders. I did not feel his body weight. I was getting to know how organisms germinated in the slush of the fields. Seban turned reptilian, he was so slimy and slippery. I was reminded of the eel that appan had caught once. Eventually, he lost his tumescence and slid off to my left side. We lay side by side like twins in a womb. Caressing the hair on my lower belly, he said lazily, 'When you grow up, you'll be hirsute like Yonachan.'

Chapter 4

The Pietà

In the arid nights after the summer rains, Malom would have Mupli beetles raining down on it. They would flow out from under the dry leaves in the estates like whirlwind. Every source of light got blanketed by the dark swarm.

'They are devil seed. Creatures that don't need to feed,' my grandfather would mutter about the Mupli beetles.

In between the tiles, in the attic, under the gunny bags and utensils, on wardrobes, beneath the tables, on the bed, every place would be teeming with them. Afraid of billions of these devils with wings, everyone would switch off lights and lamps and remain silent in the darkness. The blanket of darkness against the beetle nights. Some people would knock and grate coconut shells. The beetles were supposed to be scared by the sound.

Adhikarathil estates and orchards were the sprawling breeding grounds of the darkling beetles with chitinous exoskeletons and internal bodies only as big as a rice grain.

Two of our hills were cashew orchards. Thiruvithamkoor cultivars of rubber trees—of which five yielded one sheet of rubber—occupied the rest of the land. The beetle eggs remained dormant under the fallen leaves.

As soon as the first rains fell, the eggs hatched. As soon as they grew wings, they flew out, heading for sources of light. Daytime was spent in hiding. Until the phenolic secretions in their tiny bodies dried up and they died, they hid from sunlight and flew towards sources of other light as soon as the sun set.

My appan used to say that the Paniyas and Karimpalas were like Mupli beetles; though they worked on the land, they were rarely seen. Only when my appan and grandfather were not around did they approach the supervisors to collect their wages. My grandfather was not particularly fond of the sight of the dark-skinned workers. He insisted that his workers should be fair-skinned.

My cousin Sunny chettayi liked my grandfather's mulishness in the matter of skin colour. When wanderlust struck him, Sunny chettayi would turn up in his open-top, cut-chassis jeep. Smoking cigarettes, he would shoot the breeze with the workers. When I would try to creep up and listen in, he would chase me away with, 'Scram, kids still not out of their nappies! Get lost!'

Rubber tapping had been stopped. With clay plastered over their grooves like bandages, the trees were undergoing rejuvenation. I walked through the estate and climbed the hill to take a look at our honey beehive boxes. Adhikarathil estate was an expansive confinement home—the breeding grounds for all the crows, foxes, porcupines, hares, wild fowl, monitor lizards, squirrels and mongooses of Malom.

The birthing place of diversities . . . animals of prey, shitters, sleepers, mating pairs, gambolling bucks, suckling mothers, preening and nesting fowls, lugubrious creatures, winners, losers . . .

When I crossed the stream that cut through the length of our estate and climbed up on to the bank, I saw some movement near a gully which was hidden by the leaves of white turmeric plants. My eyes fell upon a pair of hairy, stout, fair buttocks. When I went close, I made out that the naked man lying prone was Sunny chettayi. Worried that something had happened to him, I hurried towards him.

As I looked on, it seemed like he had four legs. In between his thick, hairy legs, were a pair of candle-like fair legs.

'Sunny chettayi,' I called out.

'What do you want?'

He got to his feet looking sheepish. Beneath him was Mercy, trying to pull down her skirt below her waist. The fair-skinned housemaid of the Adhikarathil family. I was surprised she had not been suffocated to death.

'We were digging up the turmeric to make pickles.' Chettayi's explanation came without any prompting from me.

'Why did you come here?' Chettayi asked me as he fastened the mundu around his waist.

'Just like that.'

'You're straying too much these days.' Suddenly I was the offending party.

Nevertheless, after that incident, I qualified to be a listener to his tales.

When he was in the company of Emily chechi, his sister studying in Bangalore, he was a different person—a brother who was a stern guardian. However, she never cared for his style of tutelage. Every time she came to the tharavad, she stayed for three or four days. My mother treated her like her own daughter. She would describe her life in Bangalore. I got a taste of life in big cities from her descriptions. I would watch her narrate her stories. One could see the sights of the city reflected in her wide eyes.

'Emily Talkies' was what I called her. Among all my cousin sisters, this one with a movie screen for eyes was my favourite. Emily chechi loved movies. She was the one who would pursue my appan to go to the movies. My grandfather and grandmother were not fond of watching movies.

Sunny chettayi would also be with us as we drove in appan's Ambassador car to the New India movie theatre in Malom. When he got in, he seemed to fill the car. We would reach before the movie started. As a prelude to the movie, songs were played on the PA system and the first song to be played was 'Sabarimalayil Thangka Suryodayam'. The owner and workers were acquaintances of appan. We would get seated even before the tickets were bought. Later, appan would buy the tickets, and unshelled peanuts and *murukku* for snacking.

On most occasions, it used to be a full house. Only first class had cushioned seats. The second class had hard benches with backrests and the third class had plain benches without backrests. Wooden stakes driven into the ground were the demarcation between the classes.

A slide with folded hands and 'Namaste' written beneath was always the first one. Next came a picture of a cigarette crossed out in red and the legend 'No Smoking'. This was followed by a picture of a pair of legs on a seat and the legend 'Behave decently'. The whole audience would clap when the 'Namaste' slide came on. Next on the agenda were men in the audience smoking and keeping their legs on top of the seat in front.

Before the feature movie started, there would be more slides, starting with 'Adhikarathil Spices Trading'. In the slide that read 'Ponnuchami Bricks Trading', a thin, dark man in a red shirt, yellow trousers and sunglasses was featured—Ponnuchami himself. That was enough to set off catcalls. Ponnuchami did not trade in bricks. He was only a worker in the kiln. He was fulfilling his dark desire to be a movie star through that depiction of himself.

On Thursdays, families avoided coming to the movie theatre. The audience reached the movie hall keeping in the shadows and without drawing attention to themselves. They would enter the hall only after the movie started. There were cases when, in the dark of the theatre, father and son sitting adjacent to each other, asked for a light for their beedis.

My first Thursday movie was seen in the company of Sunny chettayi. As I neared the talkies, the thumping of my heart increased.

'Let's not do it, chettayi,' I bleated.

'Come on, kid.'

He purposely took tickets in the front stall since none of our acquaintances were likely to be there. Squatting on the bench with no backrest, he leaned against the wooden stakes that made up the boundary between the second class and front row and lit a beedi. He thrust one into my hand too. 'Take a drag.'

Permission received. When I placed it on my lips and lit it, it was my waist that caught fire. With each drag, the flame waxed and waned. The opening titles were enough to give me a hard-on.

A girl and a boy, lone survivors of a plane which crashed into the sea, reached an island. Someone from the audience, alive to the possibilities, shouted, 'Grow up fast, my children.'

Just as he wished, they grew up quickly. They were still in their baby clothes. They chased each other on the beach, rested in the tree shade, ate coconuts, fruits and berries, and slept in a grass hut. Everything except what the audience was expectantly waiting for happened.

Many of them hurled abuses at the hero, called him names, explained graphically what they would have done if they were in his place.

Their first attempt at sex happened twenty-three minutes after the start of the movie. The audience fell silent. The sound of a pin drop would have sounded like a cannon shot. When the hero embraced the heroine, the screen went dark. No catcalls happened. They all knew why it went dark.

The screen brightened. The hero and heroine were standing apart; both were completely naked. Next came scenes I had never seen on the screen in my life.

Out of the darkness came a question, 'Chathu sir, how is the fucking?'

Chathu sir was the social studies teacher at Malom school. His short stature had earned him the moniker Pookutti Chathu.

His students kept shooting questions at him on the quality of the action on the screen. Unable to suffer it any longer, he walked out. One of his students, an old hand at this, reminded him graciously, 'Don't go now sir, there's more humping on the way.'

Although their teacher left, his students watched all the action that continued without an intermission. When the screen went dark and brightened for a third time, everyone clapped heartily.

'Good show . . . money's worth.'

The movie went back to the air-crash survivors. Some spectators left the hall. Sunny chettayi caught hold of my hand and said, 'Come da, let's go.'

'No, let's find out if they'll get rescued, chettayi.' I was anxious.

'What the hell, as if you have come to follow the story of the bit movie.'

Clutching my hand, he dragged me out of the movie hall before anyone recognized us.

We reached home through various routes that only chettayi knew. Subsequently, I discovered my own routes to reach the theatre on Thursdays.

When I went to the movies along with my family, the ticket checker would look at me and smile meaningfully. I pretended not to see him and walked into the dark interior of the talkies.

Emily chechi would laugh and cry aloud while watching movies. While returning after watching *Gandhinagar Second Street*, she kept laughing, recalling the character who had blackened himself to look like a burglar. Although everyone in the car ribbed her for not controlling her laughter, they too laughed when reminded of that character.

Amid our laughter, Sunny chettayi asked out of the blue, 'When he appeared as the burglar, he resembled our Yonachan, didn't he, aunty?'

Appan applied the brakes suddenly. The car shuddered and swerved. My father gave Sunny chettayi a hard stare.

No one laughed after that. No one spoke either. No one had dinner too and everyone went straight to bed. I could hear my father scolding my mother for something.

Chettayi had dumped a Yonachan in the midst of our mirth. I felt he was an ogre who was standing outside our window. A masked face with a short, dark, oiled and hairy body. Who was he . . .?

I knew the Mankuruni Yonachan who had emerged from the Womb in Karikkottakkary. But why should my father become annoyed at the mention of his name?

Happiness had always been short-lived in the Adhikarathil family. I tried to recall the happy times that my father, mother and I had had together. Very rare. Are we steeped in unknown anxieties and wallowing in their depths? We surfaced occasionally only to breathe. Individual pleasures enjoyed in solitude.

For me—an occasional visit to Karikkottakkary; Seban; Thursday movies; weeklies of Kunjettan; Sunny chettayi's risqué tales.

How and when does amma breathe?

Try as I might, I could not recall how she did. Some fishes are bottom feeders. With no singular happiness.

My mother's face resembled that of Mater Dolorosa in the white-coloured Pietà installed below the crucifix of the Malom Church. Not even once was my mother cross with me. She had used her tears to mark out my path for me.

Her white arms were always around me—when we got into the Chaitra Vahini River to bathe; when, in the company of lightning and thunder, tearing out its tethers, the high wind reached us through the mountain pass; while looking out of the window at the leafless sunshine, after a bout of fever . . . she always held me close.

If my amma was Pietà, my appan was St George. The mounted, moustachioed dragon-slayer with the reared-up steed and spear aimed at the fire-breathing, scaly dragon.

He had many avenues for happiness. Hunting trips into Kodagu forests; the fish hunt along the Chaitra Vahini River; the president and head of the procession on the Feast Day of the Malom Church. The cashew water, a euphemism, was what made appan ready for all these—the firewater distilled from cashew fruits under his own supervision.

On certain evenings during the cashew season, appan and his workers would leave for the orchard, carrying brands and torches. Bright-coloured cashew fruits harvested and spread on the enormous rock in the orchard would be gathered into a reed basket. A broad areca nut spathe would be placed beneath the basket. One of the workers would step into the basket and stomp and tread on the fruits to release the juice.

Through the gaps in the reed, the juice would flow and collect in the spathe. One end of the spathe was fitted into a conduit of split bamboo which led into a cement vat placed at the foot of the rock. The blue-tinged sappy juice would keep flowing till the vat was filled to the brim.

A flat stone was placed as the lid to keep away lizards and insects. It was left to ferment for three days. The maturity of the wash could be checked by sliding the lid off and feeling it between fingers. The wash, which would have lost its froth, would be poured into a vat using a bucket. A wooden drain vessel was kept inside the straining vessel inside the copper vat. Above the copper vat was the vessel for keeping water. All the joints would be sealed with cow dung or clay.

The end of the drain vessel would stick out. To that, a reed was attached. The water on the top vessel was changed every time it started to become warm. The vapour hitting the cold bottom of that vessel condensed and fell into the strainer and seeped out through the drain vessel and then through the long reed pipe swathed in cloth, which was cooled regularly by wetting it. A large vessel was placed at the end of the long reed. When the vapour that travelled up from the vat got condensed and flowed through the reed pipe and dropped into the vessel, my appan's eyes would sparkle and his face brightened up.

'This is pristine stuff. Adhikarathil's stuff.'

He would drink a glass of the stuff, lukewarm. The rest of it would be filled into bottles and buried in the ground. It was the annual stock for my appan and my grandfather. Some of the supervisors were also given a share.

Cashew fruit arrack makes even the sweat of the drinker smell of cashew. From then on, appan's nights would start to smell of cashews. When Sunny chettayi returned after trips in his jeep, he too would have the cashew smell. One late evening, the smell of cashew lingering in the air, Sunny chettayi asked me, 'Do you want to watch the bathing scene of our actress in person?'

Malom had its movie actress too—Kavitha, daughter of Elappara Leelamma. Both made occasional visits to Ernakulam to act in movies. A liquor contractor from Kannur used to ferry them. Kavitha had acted in a movie named *Malayathi Pennu*.

We went on foot. There is a sunken lane that goes past Kavitha's home, about two feet below the level of her plot. If one crouches in that moat, one can see whatever goes on in her yard. Next to their kitchen is a low mud wall. She took her bath in the narrow yard between the house and the mud wall, which could be viewed only from a specific spot in that lane. I complimented Sunny chettayi in my mind for discovering the vantage point.

By the time we reached there, the actress had got into the yard and started to undress. The naked bulb in the kitchen threw enough light to leave nothing to the imagination. Keeping her in my sights, I stepped into the lane.

'Asshole, don't fucking stomp on me,' someone muttered.

I focused my eyes; in the pale light, I could see all the young men of Malom were arrayed there in multiple tiers. Only one of the hands was visible and unoccupied.

As the bath started in all its glory, all breathing inside the moat stopped. I witnessed hissy, steamy scenes inspired by it. The missing hands moved at commendable speed. Each sigh signified its owner was spent.

Workhorse Vakkan, who always sighed the last, looking at the moat that ran beside Elappara Leelamma's house, flooded by the millions of seeds of Malom's youth, said, 'When summer rains come, they will all be born as frogs. And when we walk through this place, they will croak, "*Appa, appa.*"'

'Ayy, no,' Sunny chettayi said, 'not frogs. They'll turn into *yakshis*, *chaathans* and *pisachas*.'

When we were returning, another smaller group of people was headed to the moat. They were Leelamma's admirers.

As we walked, I asked, 'Sunny chettayi, who's this Yonachan . . .?'

He stopped; I did too. He looked at me for some time and resumed walking and said nothing. I ran after him and repeated the question.

'Someone from Karikkottakkary,' was his non-committal reply.

'What's his connection with us?'

'He was a worker in your estate before you were born. He was fired by your grandfather for some reason. Uncle decided we'll have no more darkies after that.' Sunny chettayi was prevaricating.

'Where is he now?' I asked, making myself believe that I had not met him.

'In Karikkottakkary.'

When I heard that, I put two and two together and got five. Possibly the calculations were wrong.

What if they weren't? If they were, what does that make me? Who's the hooch-maker Mankuruni Yonachan, who hides in the Womb, to me?

After a little reflection, I wiped away all my misgivings forever. Or else, I would not have remained alive.

That year, as part of the procession of the Malom church festival, a tableau was presented on the rear of a Tempo truck—Pietà, the Sorrowing Mother Mary with the corpse of Christ on her lap. Elappara Leelamma had taken the role of the Blessed Virgin Mary. The timber loader Kora Tommy was Jesus Christ. On the bumpy ride, the corpse's head rubbed against certain sensitive areas of the Sorrowing Mother. The tickled Sorrowing Mother managed to control her laughter with great effort. The public, watching a sorrowing mother trying to control laughter, was baffled.

Thereafter, whenever I saw the Pietà, I was reminded of Leelamma. After that, I stopped gazing at the statue.

I passed my pre-degree examinations that year. Since there was nothing else to do, I joined an undergraduate course in history at the same college. I dived into the history written in the books to keep my own history, which I had wiped off from my memory, from resurfacing.

Ancient, Middle Ages, Modern, World, Indian, Kerala, human history during interstitials of ages and regions. The evolution of humans from hominids to homo sapiens. Dark men, hunter-gatherers, farmers, stone-age men, clay-potters, men who discovered black was beautiful. Ancient history was my favourite.

I imagined a human community that had remained primitive. Everyone in the classroom was naked. The history teacher Sister Ann Teresa, a female ape, was turning pages of the history text, in a primordial cave room. Scratching our heads, baring our teeth, chewing on wild roots, dozing, chasing mates, scratching sores and fondling organs, we sat around.

The moon rose in a minatory mood. Spears held aloft, chanting hunting hymns, ducking and weaving through the undulating foliage of the forest, sensing the stirrings of a boar in the darkness, stealthily closing in on the prey; the hunting circle converges to a spear point. The instinctual dash of the boar to save its life. The thrust of the hungry spears; they plunge in and come out and plunge in again and swing up. The boar is in mid-air like an inverted porcupine.

The taste of the warm swine blood; the smell of the sliced meat; the sputter of the fat bursting in the fire. Slapping off the cinders, a piece of meat is popped into the mouth and chewed on. Preparing for a nap on the warm rock. A mate calls, legs spread. Biting the lips that smelled of boar fat. Sucking on breasts that smelled of milk. Parting the legs to see the wetness between the legs . . .

'Eranimos Philippose,' the female ape called. 'What did we discuss about why the European nations vied with one another to discover a sea route to India? Pay attention.'

Sea routes, armadas, and military campaigns were subjects of discussion in the class. Voyages of the White men to discover the Black people's lands. Irrespective of the place and time, the kings were all white. Administrative reforms of the fair-skinned; their art and culture; their commercial ties; their religion and rituals; their tax systems; their currency . . .

My head became increasingly bowed. I was facing humiliation for being born dark in a family of fair-skinned people. At the church, I prayed, 'I want nothing O Lord, merely turn my complexion white like that of my family.'

I raised my head to look at the gods. All the saints were gleaming white. The tortured and crucified Jesus Christ wearing the crown of thorns was white. On the altar, I did not see a single saint who had suffered the torment of being dark-skinned.

God rejected my prayers. He must be fond of Sunny chettayi's prayers. On the days we had service, he would turn up as a supercharged devotee. He would kneel in front of the altar and belt out hymns and prayers without a break. Even the priests would be in a trance as the torrent of his words engulfed them. I asked him once, 'How do you turn so devout like this?'

'Half a bottle of the cashew arrack; no more, no less. That's the prescribed dosage for devoutness,' he laughed.

His tales were as glib as his prayers. As soon as they heard his preamble—'From the time of our forefathers, legends have sprouted in Adhikarathil orchards like rampant weeds. The story under advisement is the one that took place in Uncle Pylee's cashew orchard'—people perked up.

'The protagonist is Chembarathikkal Iype, the stud of the family; the heroine Centipede Mercy.'

'Didn't he marry her?' someone in the audience piped up.

'You swine, this story is before he married her. Don't interrupt and spoil a good story.

'During the previous cashew season, Uncle Pylee sent his army of workers into the inexhaustible orchard overrun by Siam weed plants. Even if they worked till sundown without a break, cashew nuts still remained to be picked. Men worked on one valley and the women on the other side. It was backbreaking, intense work.

'In the afternoon, Uncle Pylee downed the shutters of his shop and went up the hill. The picking had resumed after the noon break. When he counted the workers, two were short—Iype and Mercy. Uncle Pylee thought something was amiss and set out in search. He found them below the Karadi Rock, exerting themselves on each other, on a makeshift bed of Siam weed leaves. Uncle Pylee stood watching them for a while. They showed great commitment to the task at hand. Finally, wounded to the core, he asked . . .'

'What did he ask?' one of the listeners piped up.

'"Iype, I must pay you the wages for this too, I presume?"' Sunny chettayi came to the moral of the story.

'Have you all seen that after their marriage too, Mercy would pluck Siam weed leaves and take them with her? Have you wondered why? Iype can get a hard-on only if he gets its smell in the bed.'

When we were getting back after this narrative, I asked Sunny chettayi, 'When you smell white turmeric, what do you feel?'

Laughing aloud, he slapped me playfully.

Chapter 5

The Holy Week

Seban had grown. A few hairs could be seen on his upper lip, near the corners of his mouth. A few golden down hairs on his plump, shiny black torso. I had noticed all this when we had sat to decide what we should do after completing the pre-degree course. In between, Seban went inside and emerged wearing a jacket and hat. 'How do I look?' he asked.

Like a beetle standing upright.

'Well, you look like an Englishman.'

'I want to speak fluent English.' He said that in English and spoke with a dreamy look in his eyes. If he were to speak the language fluently, Father Nickolaus would send him abroad.

Based on the decision taken that day, Seban joined the BA English course in our college. His class was adorned by the beauty of Soumya C. Chacko. Once he sketched her face in a notebook. Her wide eyes were shown gazing at me lovingly. Pictures always lie. I was discovering for the first

58

time that Seban had the skill to create falsehood. I kissed the fingers that had awakened me with their caresses in the Sultan Cave.

Belying Seban's hopes, no one learnt proper English pronunciation in the college. The teachers only tried to swim across the lake of the English language without creating any ripples. With all their thoughts formed in Malayalam, the students recited *The Rime of the Ancient Mariner* in a metre used in Malayalam. By the time Father Kalayathumkuzhi was done with it, the rousing speech of Mark Antony resembled a homily from the pulpit. Seban, seeing Shakespeare through the eyes of Father Kalayathumkuzhi, opined, 'Rajan Chinnangath is a far superior writer than Shakespeare.'

We were acquainted with Rajan Chinnangath's work while still in our pre-degree class. Seban's father was a good reader. His library was a wooden plank placed over a pair of laterite blocks. Weekly magazines were arranged neatly like bar diagrams, labelled with their names—*Mangalam, Chempakam, Janani, Manorama, Sakhi*. The heights of the bars were similar; the authors in them were also not different—Mathew Mattom, Battan Boss, Josy Vagamattom, Kamala Govind, C.V. Nirmala, Joicee, Rajan Chinnangath.

Two or three weeks of reading was enough to turn me into a devotee of Vedikunjettan's cache of magazines. Every week I felt suffocated by the reverses that the handsome protagonists and gorgeous maidens had to undergo.

A trip every week to Seban's home was out of the question. I needed to be up-to-date with the weekly vicissitudes of the beautiful and handsome protagonists in the serial stories. That was how I started to procure the weeklies from the kiosk run by Titus in Malom. The stack of magazines that I had thus procured without the knowledge of my appan grew under the cover of a large copper vessel in our attic. I too became a librarian.

Emily chechi must have come to know of the existence of this secret library when she asked me, 'Do you have anything to read . . .?'

She had come from Bangalore for her holidays. I showed her my secret cache. She was thrilled. She picked up six or seven magazines and devoured them.

When my grandmother saw Emily chechi reading the magazines, she too wanted to get a piece of the action. I plied her with a few. I watched her sieve the words through the lenses of her spectacles, chew on them slowly, and ingest them. She was in the tharavad, silent, as someone who had given up on everyday life. Her presence was noticed by the others only on special occasions.

Confined to a room, seated on her chair or lying on the bed, the aged matriarch of Adhikarathil tharavad killed time. Occasionally, like someone waking up from a year-long slumber, my grandmother would get up and take a stroll through the grounds.

Like an alert mongoose, her head would be flipping in all directions. She would not miss any of the fallen and mature fruits. Ripening bird's eye chillies turning coffee brown; dried coconuts lying on the ground; ripe poovan bananas pecked at by birds; guavas brought down by the sharp claws of bats; windfall peppercorns bunches; water rose apples; custard apples—everything was picked up and stacked on the half wall of the house.

My grandfather was not as tall or fair as my father. His power came from his words. Enunciated with precision and peremptory, his words would swoop down, concise and indisputable, embellished by the grandeur and power of the Adhikarathil tharavad.

On rare occasions, my grandfather would also go for a stroll. Even if a gold ingot was lying on his path, he would not bend down and pick it up. He would ignore all windfalls and walk ahead. He was afraid that old age would play tricks on him. He dreaded old age more than he did death. He feared that it would enfeeble his words, upend the coherence of his memories, and blur his thoughts. His prayers were to go past it, the earliest possible.

During Sundays and days of obligation, my grandfather and grandmother would walk to the church together. No one else would show the temerity to occupy the seats reserved for the elders of the Adhikarathil family. All the benches with backrests were donated by our family. Not merely the benches, the reredos of St Sebastian; the carved wooden door of the sacristy with seven three-dimensional angels and ornamental lock; the public address system; the Eucharist table with its backdrop of The Last Supper—everything of note in the church was a donation of the Adhikarathil family.

Great-granddad Kuncheriya had obtained permission from the Bishop in Kozhikode to build the church in Malom. He had donated the land too. The church was built with timber and stones from Adhikarathil lands. It was truly our family church. The presidency of the church was conferred by the Bishop on the family.

The last presidency held by my grandfather during
the church festival was in the year when I was a student
of the ninth standard. As he walked at the head of the
procession holding the tall silver candle stand, the nobility
of the Adhikarathil lineage that had been distilled and passed
through the many generations shone on his face brighter
than the flame in his hand. The procession that started from
the portals of the church would wend its way through Malom
town and terminate at the shamiana near the Adhikarathil
cupola. Today, as it was then, the most prominent parade in
Malom is the church festival procession.

The procession comprised *chenda* players led by Malayan
Kunjiraman *chettan* and his sons; maidens dressed as angels
holding lamps; religious tableaus; music band players of the
Devamata band of Karikkottakkary; Luthiniya hymns sung
by Jose chettan from a jeep with speakers fastened to its roof;
devotees holding candles; the vicar holding the relic under
a canopy held aloft by four custodians; the Adhikarathil
president with his silvery wig and silver candlesticks; the
commoner presidents; and the swan-shaped carriage with
the icon of the St Sebastian—in that order.

The procession was proceeding solemnly. A sudden gust
of wind blew out my granddad's candle. I was walking ahead
of the vicar, carrying my own candle. I ran back and lit his
candle. He smiled at me. I ran back to my position ahead
of the relic but shortly heard the vicar screaming. When
I looked back, what I saw was the vicar throwing down
the relic and pulling off his stole and other vestments. The
fire had spread to his cassock. The people around him were
trying to extinguish the fire by beating it. My grandfather
stood frozen holding the silver candle sticks from which the

candles had fallen. That was the first occasion of old age throwing a scare into the Adhikarathil karanavar.

For two days, seated in the darkness of his room, my granddad spoke to no one. From the darkness wrought by his seething thoughts, he called out to my grandmother occasionally. She brought him broken-rice gruel in a bell-metal *kindi*.

A murder of crows descended on the guava tree outside his room and perched on its branches, cocking their heads to the side. My grandmother threw gravel at the crows, shouting imprecations. However, the crows did not return to the nests they had built on the rubber trees in the Adhikarathil estates. My granddad sat staring at the crows through the window, showing little emotion, although their constant cawing was making him uneasy.

My father summoned the priest. He sat in front of my granddad with Holy Water in a plastic bottle and the stole around his neck. The crows fell silent. They cocked their heads a little more and tried to listen to what the priest was saying.

The priest placed his hand on my granddad's head. He drew the cross on his temple dabbing the Holy Water. Then he made everyone leave the room. My granddad's mutterings and the priest's counters could be heard outside the room. The door opened and my granddad's face had cleared up a little. That night, when the crows returned to their nests, he called my father to his side.

'Pylee, from now on I shall not take the president's position. As the next in line, you should assume that position now.'

My father said nothing and bowed his head. Granddad placed his hand on his head. For all the festivals thereafter, the president from the Adhikarathil family was my father.

The tender coconut fronds meant for Palm Sunday also came from our lands. On Lazarus Saturday, after the arrival of our relatives, the ceremony for bringing down the fronds would start. Pappettan chose the twelve sturdy, straight palms from which the bunched-up tender leaflets were cut and brought down. The candle was lit in front of the Sacred Heart icon on the portico and the leaf bunches were placed next to it.

As soon as the prayers were over, my father took up the bunches, loaded them on to the jeep and headed for the church. The sexton and his helpers would separate the leaflets and cut them to equal lengths. Each leaflet had a fantail made of smaller leaflets at one end, and they were hung up to decorate the altar.

On that Palm Sunday, the sunrise had taken on a hue of tender coconut leaflets. The entire parish was present in the church. The consecrated tender leaflets had to be sent to each family, one for each member. Till they were burnt to ashes on Ash Wednesday as the start of Lent, forty-eight days before the completion of a year, as sacramentals they ensured the prosperity and welfare of the family.

On that Palm Sunday, when the congregation overflowed, the believers knelt on the ground, under the shade of the trees. The vicar and the deacons stood with the bundles of the palm leaflets in the middle of the church.

The swirling, palm-waving devotees moved out in ripples from the priests and flowed into the open grounds. Everyone held a palm leaflet in their hand. The yellowness, width and the three 'V's embossed at the bottom were indicators of auspiciousness. Each of them inspected their leaflet to evaluate their holiness. Those who received green and damaged leaflets were disappointed. Those with thin leaves let out sighs of disappointment.

I received the most auspicious-looking leaflet. As we set off on the palm leaf procession, I held it close to me. When I could smell pollen that had gathered on the palm leaf, I had this random thought—Nature enters the church so profusely only on Palm Sundays.

How did the olive leaves of Jerusalem become coconut palm leaflets in Kerala? In the Parayas' dance called Parayanthullal and Kalamezhuthu for serpent worship, palm leaflets were used as an adornment. Theyyam, too, was partial towards tender palm leaves. In the shrines and groves of Kali, for animal sacrifices, this was essential. Do they use these leaves in the big temples run by the caste Hindus?

By the time the palm leaf procession went around the church thrice, the sexton would be rushing around, closing all the doors from inside.

Next was the entry of Jesus Christ into Jerusalem.

'*Lift up your heads, O you gates! Lift up, you everlasting doors! And the King of glory shall come in.*'

With a peacock feather-tipped mid-rib of the coconut leaf, the vicar tapped the main door thrice chanting the spell for opening the door. On the third tap the door opened by itself. Everyone got back to the Palm Sunday prayers.

It was my duty to cut down the banana stalks every year on Palm Sunday. My granddad believed that my luck was good with agriculture and that only if I cut down the stalks would the bananas ripen properly. Much later, only after I was past thirty years, did I realize that it was not an accolade for me.

On Palm Sunday evening, the banana stalks were lowered into a ripening pit. Using coconut husk embers and dried cow-dung, the pit was turned into a smoke chamber. The pit was sealed using wooden planks and clay. The pit was unsealed on Maundy Thursday morning. Perspiring golden ripe bananas could be seen in the smoke-filled pit.

The summer rain had come in its full glory on that Maundy Thursday. The garlic kept for drying the previous day got wet. The Mupli beetles swarm arrived in search of light. For three days it rained in the evening. The water carried dried cashew fruits and dry leaves into the fields.

When the Pesaha appam—the Passover Bread—was being cut, the rains strengthened. My Pana recitation was drowned by its sounds.

My father said, 'No one will leave now. The wind and rain are getting worse.' Johnny pappan seconded it. Sunny chettayi turned up late for the Pesaha appam cutting. After everyone else had fallen asleep, I asked him, 'So you did watch the Thursday movie?'

'Ah yes. *Sankarankutty Needs a Girl*. Among the best adults-only movies I have seen,' he said with obvious relish.

With appropriate gestures and actions, he narrated the amorous conquests of the short, dark-skinned protagonist Sankarankutty who had a deformed arm. He claimed that the appam-cutting ceremony was likely to be delayed in most of the houses in Malom that night.

The narration ended only after everyone had retired. As I was moving towards the bedroom, dejected at having missed the erotic movie, chettayi told me, 'I want to sleep alone tonight. I'll sleep here.' He pulled out the throw from the sofa, spread it on the floor, and lay down in the hall.

When I switched on the light in my room, Emily chechi said softly, 'Switch it off. It will attract the beetles.' She was lying on my bed.

I switched off the light. I lay down beside her. My mind was full of Sankarankutty's exploits. When the rains strengthened outside and coolness drifted in, she embraced me. Her lips, which smelt of Inri appam, were right in front of my nose. When my nostrils flared drinking in that smell, as if she sensed it, she parted her lips. To savour those trembling lips, I stuck out my tongue and touched them. She pursed her lips and sucked on my tongue.

She released my tongue only to whisper, 'Lock the door and come.'

When I returned after locking the door, I was a free man. And she, an unbound woman.

Man tasted woman. The tongue skimmed over stirring salinity and conquered the undertones of garlic. The room was suffused by the primal smell of reproduction that feminine odour gives off. Hands roved all over, relishing the contours of the soft flesh, reminiscent of soft, gooey clay. As lightning flashed, the eyes hungered to drink in the sights of erogenous zones denied till then. The sounds and vocalizations rendered illogical by errant, tumescent emotions made love to one's ears. We hurt each other, pinched, nibbled and nipped. Our sweat bathed the other. Moans led to arousal; sharpened the desire; deepened the orgasm.

As we lay entwined, becalmed like the morning twilight that refused to cede ground, Emily chechi asked me, 'Aren't I a sister to you?'

'No, you aren't,' I replied.

As she kept caressing my arm gently, Emily chechi was lost in thought. For the first time in my life, my bastardy came as a solace to me. Without asking any other questions, she turned towards me and silently kissed me softly, her lips forming a canopy over mine. It was an erotic stamp, liberating me from brotherhood. Had Emily chechi also considered me an interloper in the Adhikarathil family?

The next day, Good Friday, everyone went to church from the tharavad. Dressed in black vestments, the vicar stood at the altar, ready to be the sacrificial lamb.

I felt drawn to the Christ dressed in black. The crowd spat on his face and mocked him, hailing him as the king of Adhikarathil.

Should they not be hailing him as the King of Jews?

Good Friday gave one time and space to sit in the church and ponder. I watched the people around me. As they sat expressionlessly gazing at the altar, they seemed to be full of varied emotions—hatred, regret, lust, storge, sympathy, fear, devotion. The church is a place where hundreds of emotions are consecrated in a bonfire. Each individual is a firepan.

Occasionally, belches and farts spread the smell of post-digestive vapours of the previous day's diet of coconut milk and garlic-infused Passover Bread. Swinging the thurible that gave off incense fumes, the sexton chased away the plummy smell of farts to the heights of the church.

As the enactment of Christ's flagellation and torture ended on the altar, an emotional Jose chettan from the choir sang with a trill in his voice:

'The lament echoed from
Golgotha Hill:

What sin did I do
For me to be crucified?'

As the people, like the searing breeze of an elegy, flowed forward to kiss the crucifix, I, nursing pleasurable thoughts about my maiden carnal experience, tried to find Emily chechi. She was standing in the women's section, her head covered with a shawl. I placed myself in the queue so that I would reach the crucifix at the same time as chechi. We kissed the crucifix at the same instant. Chechi looked at me wide-eyed. In front of the bleeding icon of Jesus Christ, I had an erection. The oblation of bitter chiretta plant juice that I received at the portal of the church tasted saccharine to me.

In the evening, as we climbed the Kottathalachi Hill while singing the 'Way of the Cross', I walked beside Emily chechi. When we descended, the whole family was together. She walked with a hand on my shoulder. Others did not notice us moving consciously close and rubbing against each other.

My mother had cut the leftover Inri appam into slices like harmonium keys and kept them out for drying. They were placed in the kitchen on flat winnowing baskets and covered with old muslin cloth. The next day, they had to be dried in the sun. At night, as we lay down after supper, a faint smell of garlic wafted in.

Garlic is a snake repellent. I recalled the climax scene of the movie *Rathinirvedam*. It was raining in the inky serpent grove. Standing in the darkness of the serpent grove, Emily chechi and I were in a damp, tight embrace, dissolved into each other.

I tiptoed into my aunt's room, gently grazed Emily chechi's foot and gestured towards the kitchen—our serpent grove. She pulled up her anklets on to her calves to stop the bells from tinkling; with her leaning on my shoulder, we reached the grove. I spread my lungi on the floor, to make it our imaginary *sarppakkalam*. The serpents, fused by *ashtabandham*—the traditional mortar made of powdered shells, gallnut, resin, sandstone, river sand, gooseberry, lac and cotton wool, used to fix idols to their base in temples— writhed and thrashed on the sarppakkalam. The smell of Inri appam in our sweat inflamed us. Finally, when I was trying to suppress with my own lips the moans escaping from a bucking Emily chechi, whom passion was tearing apart, the lamp of the grove came on.

As we stood up in fright, we saw our granddad—as tall as the ceiling—with his eyes averted from us.

Gathering up her clothes that had been flung around, Emily chechi ran towards her room, sobbing.

My head bowed and cloaked by my black lungi, I stood in front of my granddad.

My mother came in, woken up by the sounds. As she stood bewildered and unaware of what had passed, my granddad told her, 'Move away from his sight. This blackguard Pulaya doesn't care whether it's his mother or his sister . . .'

As I saw my mother fall in a faint, was my feeling one of relief? Her eyes tore into me like whiplashes. I was in agony.

The flight of stairs to my room was like climbing the Golgotha. I lay down in my room as if it was a sepulchre.

The next day, Black Saturday, my mother appeared before my vault and wept. When she heard my father's voice from downstairs, she quickly wiped her tears and went down. Through the window I saw Emily chechi leave, her eyes puffy and face swollen from crying. My mind was numb, unable to weigh right from wrong.

On Easter night, I woke up to the booming sounds of mortars being burst in the church. When I looked through the window, the yard, the walls and our lands beyond that lay in darkness. I stood up, shaking off the white sheet that I used to cover myself. I felt one with the shiny darkness that I saw. I went down the steps of the ancient staircase of the Adhikarathil family and opened the door. I walked through the crypts of darkness, heading into my own resurrection.

Chapter 6

Father Nickolaus

Seated by the side of the firepan in the Devamata Church yard, the song I sang was about dark, inky blackness. Kapli played an old triple drum keeping the tempo. Thin, mournful strains of Marangan's clarinet flowed through the melancholy of my song.

It was a night in June when the monsoon rains had stayed away. Cicadas and night fowl provided uninhibited accompaniment to my song. Kapli and Marangan stood a little away from the bonfire. For them, the warmth from the fire only grazed their skin. They resembled Latin American musicians in their trousers and jackets and hats on their heads.

Father Nickolaus was roasting a small, skewered tuber in the fire, taking care that no embers fell on his luxurious white beard. I looked at the German priest with respect as he sat rapt in the ebb and flow of the song that the Adhikarathil family reunion had rejected with derision.

The imperturbable father to a whole community and their domicile. The saint of Karikkottakkary, gently peeling the skin of a tuber, without any pretensions. In crinkly letters, the chronicles of Karikkottakkary had been etched on his wrinkled skin.

When I set off from Adhikarathil and reached Seban, I was headed for an indeterminate future. As I stood despondent with my head bowed, Seban told me, 'Father Nickolaus is the saint of new beginnings.'

Another Moses who led a people—enslaved only because of their race—to Canaan, the Promised Land of Karikkottakkary.

Father Nickolaus's first stop had been Alappuzha. He toured the backwaters and hills and valleys to Kottayam and Pala witnessing the toiling masses. The grandees among Catholics invited him for feasts where roast duck and rice dumplings were served.

The priest, however, chose to dine with the Pulayas in their hovels. Savouring tapioca and bird's eye chilli chutney in the light of bonfires built in clay pits, he listened to their laments. He encouraged them to throw off their bondage and start their own farming. The Pulayas told him that they had no land. The priest headed to Malabar to find land for them.

It was the fag end of the migration from south Kerala into Malabar. All the hills had already been cornered by the Christians. As the dejected priest was about to return, Chathunni Nambiar, the caretaker of Karikkattidam Nayanar, told him about Karikkottakkary. The priest readily agreed to take a look.

Setting off from Malom, they went past Enthumkari, Uruppukutti and climbed the Kalangki Hill. Nambiar pointed out Karikkottakkary to the priest. An expansive, fallow landscape dominated by black laterite. Lemongrass grew prodigiously on the loose soil on the laterite. Barren land that was rejected by all the Christians and Ezhavas after a single glance. The priest saw the land and the sky.

He had to provide land for all the people he would bring with him. Until the land started to give returns, they needed money to feed and clothe themselves. Money was needed for transportation and farming. He totted up the money in hand and what the Church may grant him. Finally, the Good Lord decreed. The Promised Land of the Pulayas was this one indeed.

The landowner charged nothing for that rocky, barren land. The priest paid Chathunni Nambiar a gratuity for being his guide. He cut the branches of the ironwood tree, tied it with vines, and erected a crucifix in the centre of Karikkottakkary. Later that became the site for the Devamata Church.

When he was back in Thiruvithamkoor, no one believed his words. However, the thought of owning a piece of land enticed a few of them to follow the cross.

Father Nickolaus believed unquestioningly that all the security in his life, from his birth in the village of Mittenwald in Germany to that day had been the benediction of the Christian path that he followed. To take with him to Malabar, he chose only the few who wore the devotional scapular and bowed their heads to be baptized.

The sight of the barren Karikkottakkary baffled the men. They muttered and griped about the padre. They got ready to return. The padre got them together and conducted prayers. The Pulayas were introduced to the God of the padre during that prayer—the God who brought forth clear springs in the desert; the God who fed thousands manna and locusts; the God who changed water into wine. They too started to believe in that God.

That God blessed the Pulayas. Each family was given three acres of land. They received bamboo and thatch to build huts, implements to till the land, and saplings and seeds to plant. When they were hungry, they were given cornflour, broken wheat, milk powder, soyabean oil and fish oil that America had sent them. Used garments from Europe clothed them.

That was the beginning of human habitation in Karikkottakkary. Its people drank tea lightened by milk powder in the mornings; for their elevenses, they had corn meal upma made in soya bean oil; lunch was broken-wheat gruel with fish powder chutney; supper was steamed corn meal balls and fish oil. The men wore trousers and jackets; the women frocks and gowns. Under the aegis of a munificent Father Nickolaus, a primitive community flourished, living like Westerners.

The Pulayas tamed the barren land, under the aegis of Father Nickolaus. The first battle was with the lemongrass that grew taller than them. They descended on the lemongrass swathes as they would on the paddy fields at Pokkali. They tried to distil the grass in copper vats. In the beginning, the vats got burnt; and the oil evaporated. Gradually, they sussed out the amount of water to be used; the calories to be applied; the cooking levels of the grass. The lemongrass oil in the Pulayas' bottles turned out to be the most fragrant.

The lemongrass harvest revealed the dark topsoil. That set the Pulayas' hearts racing. Without any prompting from the padre, they descended onto the earth. They sowed paddy; planted cashew, mango, jackfruit trees and coconut palms in the gaps between laterites. Mexican lilac staffs were driven into the ground as support for black pepper vines. Whatever the Pulayas touched turned to gold. They felt a happiness they had never experienced before. One's own tapioca, paddy, banana plants, one's own land . . .

No one came to lord over them. It was the realm of the blacks. No racial slurs, no humiliation citing the colour of the skin. When news of the Promised Land reached them, many of their neighbours and relatives from Thiruvithamkoor started to land up in Karikkottakkary. The padre distributed as much land as he could to the new arrivals.

The people of Karikkottakkary obeyed their liberator Father Nickolaus unconditionally. Heeding his words, they built the church; then they built the school; in the summer, when they ran out of water, they dug wells at the four corners of Karikkottakkary and one smack in the middle of it. These wells, sixty to seventy-five feet deep, filled up with clear water as springs seeped in through fissures and bores.

A polytechnic institute was started so that young men could have vocational training as mechanics and carpenters. That grew into the Devamata Industrial Training College. To keep their earnings from farming secure and to extend loans, the Karikkottakkary Thrift Society was started. It grew into the Karikkottakkary Co-operative Bank. For students who failed the tenth-class public examination and those who wanted to study further, a non-regular college was started. Before he attained the hallowed serenity of the old age, Father Nickolaus had transformed Karikkottakkary.

He had a certain vision not merely about their material well-being, but what Karikkottakkary should be spiritually too—an unsullied, dyed-in-the-wool Christian community. He taught his flock to light candles in the late evenings and count the rosary. He educated them so that they could read and learn the hymns. He taught them how to celebrate Christmas and Easter and observe the Lent and Maundy Thursday. He trained them in taking out processions during feasts.

He took them through the paces in volleyball, badminton, tug-of-war; he trained them in playing the musical band, singing Christian hymns, Biblical plays. However, all the while, the subconscious mind of Karikkottakkary was being enticed by some of the pleasures that had been coded into its genes and that the padre could never blot out.

At the time of leaving my home, I was not aware of the existence of Father Nickolaus. My only objective was to be in Karikkottakkary, the land of my illegitimate father.

I informed Seban, 'Whatever happened during the Holy Week was an augur. I should have been living here . . . this place has been beckoning me from the first sight . . . my dear ones are here.'

'What about the Adhikarathil family?' Seban asked.

'Who are they?'

He laughed and hugged me. 'You are from this place. And my closest relative.'

Seban's mother sent me to Father Nickolaus. I knelt in the confessional. I was not confessing my sins.

That serene ocean received calmly my anxieties, my hurts, my ignorances, my happinesses . . . all my confessions, shorn of the froth of sin, that pacific ocean took in with grace. At the end, in Malayalam which still had the vestiges of his Teutonic descent, the padre spoke to me like a gentle breeze that caresses leaves.

'Son, do not be sad. There are many things beyond our control in this life of ours. Our birth, death, family, children, blood relations, future . . . we are mere beneficiaries of the rights and wrongs in these. God holds the tiller.'

After sighing deeply, he continued, 'However, for the solace of the helpless, He has given everyone a part of Himself. However, we can use that godliness only for the benefit of others. We can, to a great extent, contribute to and determine comfort, peace of mind and prosperity. We are wasting our lives without realizing the divinity that resides in us. If you need to grieve, they should not be over things that we cannot control. It should be over the divinity that we are squandering away.'

I went out of the confession box and headed for the altar. I pondered over the God that was within me. I repented that my inner God had done nothing for others.

The padre was waiting for me outside. Holding me close to him, he said, 'You have many paths to choose from. The safest would be to return to the Adhikarathil fold.'

'No, I'm not going there anymore.' I did not have to think twice.

'The other is filled with misery, with tribulations. We can't see or experience ourselves in that path. There will be only others there. The way of the godliness in you. That was the path I have trodden in the last fifty-two years.'

After I stopped singing, Marangan continued to play the clarinet.

Marangan and Kapli had both come to the padre many years ago. The family had left the two blind children in the padre's care. In the catechism classes, all the students were addressed by their first and family names. The others truncated the names of the children in the padre's care and abbreviated their family names. Thus, Marangottukottil Varghese became Marangan. Kaplikkundil Scaria became Kapli. As his eyes roved, only in a particular position could he sense a spot of light. Kapli always kept rolling his head in search of that dot of light. Marangan was not that lucky. Behind his eyelids, his eyes had shrunk so much that they were practically non-existent.

They were the padre's swineherds. At the time of the migration to Karikkottakkary, the padre had brought a pair of piglets with him. He recalled, in the Book of Exodus, the people of Israel clamouring for meat in the desert.

When his two pigs delivered litter after litter of piglets, the people in Karikkottakkary gave the padre a nickname—Panniyachan, or the Swine Priest. When he heard the name, he laughed. When his flock asked for meat, he pointed towards his drove of black pigs. Thereafter, all their festivals were redolent with the smell of pig fat.

Butchery was Vedikunju's duty. He would smash a heavy hammer down on the head of the pig. It was only when the blow landed that the pig looked up. In his death throes, looking at the sky for the first and last time, the pig would topple over.

Using a lit brand, the pig would be roasted lightly. When the hairs were fully singed, the carcass was washed in hot water. Using a razor, the skin was shaved. To prevent hair from sprouting again in the shaved areas, turmeric paste mixed with a spot of lime was applied. The pig steeped in yellow was laid on green coconut thatches and eviscerated. The entrails were pulled out and cut into four portions with a chopper.

The body, kept on a wooden block, was chopped, diced and partitioned. Every house in Karikkottakkary would get a share, for which a small sum of money had to be paid to the church. The meat was wrapped in the long leaves of the Indian laurel tree and tied up with thin banana plant fibres.

Kapli and Marangan would fetch animal offal in a wooden pail from Thekkukalayil Ambrose's butcher shop, beyond the Karikkottakkary market. They diced and cooked the offal inside a shed near the pigsty. Breaking the white layer of congealed fat that forms on the top, resembling an ice-covered sea, they fed the dark meat pieces to the pigs, who ate it slurping and smacking loudly.

Once the feeding was done, Marangan, holding his white cane, would leave for a stroll taking a now-familiar route. Kapli stayed within the perimeter of the church, chatting up the idols, lighting candles, and sweeping the place. In the night, when they retired to their room at the rear of the church, Marangan could be heard narrating his day's story in a low, muttering tone.

My room was next to that of the padre. He used to set my daily chores. Stock register of oil and cornflour brought from Kozhikode; applications for help; baptism notices; marriage certificates—I had to write them out and keep the records. I was the de facto office secretary of the church.

Two weeks after I arrived in Karikkottakkary, my appan and amma landed up. My appan did not look at me. Crying, my amma ran towards me and hugged me. My mind was numb, and I was unable to say anything to my mother.

Facing the jamun tree as if addressing it, with his back to me, appan spoke, 'You are our only child. Whatever I say now is for your sake, not for our sake. You don't need to live your life here. The Adhikarathil family has not ostracized or disinherited you.'

'I shall live with the padre here. I am not coming back to Adhikarathil.'

My mother burst into tears. I let her cry.

After finishing his *solo novena* to Our Lady of Perpetual Succour, Father Nickolaus emerged from the church. As my enraged father rushed towards him, the padre disarmed him with a child-like smile. Shepherding appan and amma towards the big mango tree, he spoke to them, quiet and serene as melting snow. When his soft voice flowed over them drenching them in coolness, they became baptized once again. Finally making the sign of the cross, Father blessed them. Before they left, my appan said to me, 'You may do as you like. If ever you feel any affection towards us, come home. The tharavad is your inheritance.'

They started to walk back. I did not pause to think why they did not hate me. The only thought in my mind was that I had become a bona fide Karikkottakkaran.

Christmas and New Year were the most important celebrations for Karikkottakkary. The twenty-five days of fasting for Lent were strictly observed. Devoid of meat, fish, eggs and milk, the dining plates of Karikkottakkary would take on a Brahminical shade. Bellies would turn frigid like ice-covered lakes and snow-covered peaks. Karikkottakkary would slip into a meditative slumber, without feasts and house visits.

Father Nickolaus had inculcated discipline and abstinence in them over many years.

On Christmas eve, the restraints of abstinence would start to loosen. Christmas carol singers, music band, bouncing Father Christmas, balloons, lamp processions, fireworks—the place would resound with revelry, lights, songs and prayers.

Every house would have its nativity scene and crèche. Fields created with shallots, mustard, and paddy grown in coconut shells; stacked pebbles resembling rocks; streams flowing down plantain leaf sheaths; bridges made with plantain petioles; humble dwellings and palaces fashioned out of cardboard; shepherds; the wise men from the East; donkeys; cows; camels; sheep; Virgin Mary; Joseph; baby Jesus. The best nativity scene in every ward was given an award.

By 10 p.m., every resident of Karikkottakkary would be present around the bonfire. At midnight, when the baby Jesus was born, the padre would fetch him and warm him at the bonfire. Baby Jesus, warmed thus, would be moved to a large manger.

This would be followed by the mass. After the mass, the padre would wish everyone Merry Christmas and retire. The public rushed back home in an unholy haste. The bells tolling after the mass would have awakened the bellies and loins that had turned gluttonous after twenty-five days of self-denial. The Christmas eve night in Karikkottakkary was best loved by its couples.

From a night of bed-wrecking lovemaking, Karikkottakkary would wake up to the sight of bloodied coconut fronds laid over its field of butchery. Buffaloes brought from Kodagu were slaughtered and flayed in the light of petromaxes under the mango trees. After the sides were cut out and sliced, the meat was apportioned among all the families. The meat, packed in teak leaves, would reach the houses before the day broke. Beef curry and appam; beef curry and tapioca; beef curry and rice. The smell of fried coriander and chillies would rise from among the boiling buffalo fat. The bottles of Yonachan's brew would find their way into the homes surreptitiously.

However much Father Nickolaus tried to tamp down on it, fights were sure to break out in most places—if not within the family, then between neighbours. It would start off as swearing that reeked of hooch and buffalo fat. It would move on to fisticuffs. But none of the fights went beyond the tug-of-war ground, where everyone shook hands, laughed and parted as friends.

All Christian families in Malom owned bell-metal vessels handed down as heirlooms. Though it had a certain sheen of tradition, they were all covered in verdigris. Karikkottakkary had no bell metal vessels, only new aluminium vessels. They were washed daily, and their newness retained. The people did the same with their own traditions.

It was my first Christmas after moving to Karikkottakkary. When the crowds had dispersed after the midnight mass, I returned to my room and prepared to go to bed. Kapli had switched off all the lights in the church and surroundings, save the one in the nativity scene and crèche. Marangan was feeling his way through, holding the pillars at the rear of the church. Picking up my flashlight, I went to him. He was holding the pillars with both his hands and seemed to be pushing something between them with his hip.

'Why are you standing here, Maranga?' My question seemed to startle him.

Only when I swung the beam towards the pillars did I see a dark girl who was bent over. Her dress had been swept up like the feathers of a peacock.

With a frown, Marangan said, 'It's the end of the fast. Erani, you go and sleep.'

Marangan's escapade without the padre knowing of it surprised me. But then, many things were happening in Karikkottakkary without his knowledge. One night when I was returning from Seban's home, near the path leading to Sultan Cave, I saw a light shining. Something that sounded like a woodpecker hammering at the tree could be heard too.

When I went up to the spot, I saw a small group of five or six men under a prickly ash tree. Atop a big boulder placed in their middle were a hibiscus flower and different types of leaves. One of them was drumming on a rather large coconut shell whose mouth had been covered by a piece of leather. Holding a bunch of leaves, another man was dancing vigorously in rhythm to the drumming, as if in a trance. Another man held a rooster in his hand and bit into its neck. The blood sprouted like a bouquet of scarlet flowers. Shaken and scared, I left the place without looking back.

Seban told me later, 'There are two things that Father Nickolaus can't ban in Karikkottakkary. One, black magic, like the scene you witnessed. Two, the Communist Party.'

In those hilly tracts, the first place where communists hoisted their flag was Karikkottakkary.

Chapter 7

Devamata Music Band

Devamata College was inside a cashew orchard, off the road and to the right of the church. The building had only a half wall made of laterite; the rest of the wall was a bamboo mat with black oil applied to it. Those who failed in their secondary school examination and could not find seats for their pre-university and undergraduate courses in Vimalagiri College ended up there. Although they had few academic qualifications to boast of, the teachers were knowledgeable people. When I had no work related to the church, I whiled away my time at the vicarage.

Possibly because he felt that I would end up lazy, Father Nickolaus appointed me as a teacher at Devamata College.

'Teach them all that you know. Don't bother about the subject or the class.' He gave me free rein.

History was the subject I liked to teach. I exhorted the young generation of Karikkottakkary to learn their own history by talking with their elders before they learnt history written in the books.

They had a new story to narrate every day. When I spoke to them of the Indus Valley civilization of the Dravidians, they spoke of their forebears who had to feed their hunger by eating gruel from small, leaf-lined pits dug in the ground their masters had them dig.

When Tipu Sultan's military campaigns were read out to them, they told me about an incident during Tipu's passage through the Pokkali fields in the erstwhile Kochi kingdom. When he and his army rode through the fields with its tall paddy stalks, they saw some naked Pulaya women—who then had no right to wear clothes—walking through the fields. Tipu, taking pity on them, took his own mantle and threw it to them. Through gestures and his own language, he conveyed to them to cover their nakedness and live like human beings.

To deter Tipu from subjugating Angamali, its people decided to breed pigs in every home, and Tipu decided that he could do without a land with thousands of pigs running loose—this was also history that I learnt from my students.

When I took classes on the French Revolution, their minds were full of angst about the helplessness of their ancestors who could not react with even a dirty look when the cruel landlord kicked down and stomped one of the Pulayas and drowned him in the swamp as punishment for his temerity for asking for some rest in the afternoon.

The young minds, wounded by the miseries visited on their ancestors, threw many questions at me. It was a world of which I had little knowledge. The questions were about the unfamiliar lives of the Pulayas, which were not recorded in any book.

In the nights, as I lay beneath the mango tree, I had visions of the past, as vast and infinite as the sky. Like the stars, the lighted spots were few and far between. It was filled with darkness. Darkness was the truth—the moans and laments and clanking of the chains of those overlooked in the dark underbelly of history.

Our history is a collection of conjectures and beliefs. It is believed that *chera* + *alam* or Cheralam (land of the Cheras) eventually became Keralam. It is believed that the Hundred Years' War happened. It is believed that there was a port called Muziris. It is believed that Cheraman Perumal went to Makkah. It is believed the Chera dynasty was the first to rule Kerala. Mere beliefs. The way I was believed to be a member of the Adhikarathil family.

A month later, the padre came to me while I was in the staff room. He picked up the books lying on the table, glanced at their covers and told me, 'The students have an important hurdle to get over. The university examination. This is not a mere belief. That is the reality. And the only reality.'

He took out old notebooks wrapped up and kept in the almirah in the staff room and handed them over to me.

'These have everything that needs to be taught. For years, students have been writing what's inside these books and receiving high marks. You merely read these out to them. They will take notes. That should suffice.'

For the first time, I felt irritated by the padre. He was old-fashioned. As ancient as the disintegrating packet of books handed over to me.

That night, as I dozed on the platform around the big mango tree, the wrinkled palm of the padre caressed my forehead.

'Son, during youth, the mind yearning for goodness would be steadfast like yours. I chose this path because once I also thought like you do now. That was God's plan. When I reached Thiruvithamkoor, I was monopolized by Christian grandees. For months together, I could see no one but these grandees. For me, the others remained in the darkness, in a kind of darkness that you can't even begin to imagine.'

I could see old memories crowd into his eyes.

'I saw them for the first time in a landlord's fields. They had more mud on them than on earthworms; more brutalized than oxen under the yoke; they had no right to wear white, starched clothes; no right to eat cooked rice; no right to light lamps; no right of access . . . they did not even know they belonged to the human race. My heart told me that Jesus should have been born here. "I tell you the truth, when you did it to one of the least of these, my brothers and sisters, you were doing it to me!" I heeded His words and did the little that I could. Son, it's when your thoughts are put into action that it becomes history. The dark history that you have seen has been limited to your thoughts. If your mind is distressed, start to act.'

That summer I started to act.

When the squabble for water started around the five wells in Karikkottakkary, the padre talked about a drinking water scheme for the place.

'You need to do this.' His challenge energized me.

I went to all the households. Eventually, we created twenty-two committees, each committee representing forty households. A general committee with representatives of each of these committees was at the helm of the

Karikkottakkary Drinking Water Project. The padre was the patron and I the convenor. The padre found some agency as the investor. When each family made a small contribution, we had a corpus.

A big tank was built on top of Kalanki Hill. Water was pumped into the tank from all the wells, and then piped into every home. When the water was insufficient, a new pond was dug, and a pump and motor installed. The Karikkottakkary drinking water scheme was accepted as the model for all the Jalanidhi and People's Planning schemes that came later.

The enthusiasm generated by the drinking water scheme flowed into many other schemes—housing scheme, a toilet for every house, biogas plants, energy-efficient stoves, micro-income schemes . . . the place prospered from the goodwill of cooperation. The public took ownership of every scheme and project. The padre acted as the arbiter and settled disputes.

My days turned busy. I started to go to bed late. I thought about myself. The bastard son of the Adhikarathil family had gone beyond the individual named Eranimos. My views were considered and acknowledged. My presence was not being ridiculed.

The paths I had taken . . . the Adhikarathil tharavad, granddad, my parents, Malom, Vimalagiri College, Seban, Sunny chettayi, Emily chechi, Yonachan, Karikkottakkary, Father Nickolaus. Karikkottakkary had made me what I was.

Seban was a bridge for me to reach Karikkottakkary. His family had brought me to Father Nickolaus.

But when I think of it, I would have reached here, whether or not Seban had come into my life, or I had met

Yonachan or not. There was a sanguinary predisposition that transcended all these personalities.

One day, Seban came to my lodgings. I suddenly realized that I had not met him for a long time.

'Seban, I'm sorry, I was preoccupied,' I apologized to him.

'Erani, in between, I had gone to till the land of Urumbayil Pappachan. That sixty-two-year-old and I were tilling together. However much I tried, he would be about eight feet ahead of me, still digging. And he had cutting things to tell me. "Sonny boy, don't try to keep up with me. Take some rest before you start again." It's the same with Father Nickolaus. Whoever's with him will be frothing from the mouth with the effort of keeping up with him.'

He became my true friend.

'Even if it's not easy going, I like this path. Don't people feel the presence of an Eranimos here? That's all I need,' I said, gratified.

'I too need to find a way for me. I have come to discuss that.' He turned serious.

'What are your plans?'

When I asked him that, he turned despondent. He spoke after a little while, 'Within Karikkottakkary, we are a model community. The same colour, the same faith, united, and economically about the same level. Hardworking people who care for one another, good people . . . To the world outside, we are still mere Karikkottakkarans. Unpedigreed new converts.' His voice had become thick.

'I have always wondered, why did my parents convert? For the Christians, we are still Pulayas. At the same time, do we get even one of the benefits that Pulayas get as a Scheduled Caste . . .?'

I interrupted him as spoke. 'Why do you feel all this now?'

'Only now have I been moving out of Karikkottakkary to attend to my needs. I realized the extent of the discrimination only when I went in search of a job. Consider this—is any convert running any institution where an educated youth can find employment? I too want to have a job like others who studied in our college have found. It's not going to happen . . . I am fed up with roaming about in search of a job. Eranimos, racial discrimination is alive and well—right in front of us. Based on the colour of our skin. Right here in Kerala. We are its victims.'

Everything he said was so cruelly true.

'This is a castle of dreams. A castle of temptations built by Christianity. When we live like old people in this palace, we feel everything is safe and secure. There is no escape from this castle. If I had not converted, I could have held my head high and claimed that I was a Pulaya. I am fed up with this life—neither here nor there. I must escape, Erani. I have found the way.'

'What's the way?' I asked.

'I found an old caste certificate in the iron trunk at home, certifying that my *achachan* was a Pulaya.'

'And using that . . .?'

'Let me see what I can do with it. There's only one person who can understand me, and that's you. That's why I have come to you.'

Seban had become a grown-up suddenly. Someone capable of cutting his own path in life.

'I'll need your help in many things,' he reminded me again when he was leaving. Not wanting to let him leave in a sombre mood, I asked him, 'All that will be done. Do you have any news on our Soumya C. Chacko?'

'You have not been able to forget her, eh?' he still looked grim.

'I had forgotten all about her. You brought back her memories,' I said a white lie.

'Is that so?' he laughed and walked towards the bus stop. Perhaps because the bus reached then, he said nothing more.

One Sunday, after the public meeting at the church, when we were having our lunch, the padre asked me, 'Don't you want to learn to play in the music band?'

'Oh, isn't it a bit hard, padre?' My heart wasn't in it.

'Son, nothing is achieved without hard work. It's the best occupation for those who have an ear for music and have the strength.'

What he said was true. Devamata Band was putting the food on the table for fifteen families of Karikkottakkary.

'Whether you get trained in being a member or not, from today onwards you have to take care of the band.'

He had foisted on me another responsibility. Devamata was the biggest music band in the whole region. The bandmaster was Nalampudam Lazar *asan*. The padre never went to the bandmaster. Lazar never remained anywhere where the padre could see him. He always trailed the smell of hooch in his wake.

He was always dressed in a flowery lungi and red jacket and wore his long grey hair in a plait. Since he never unplaited his hair, it had become matted. Every season he would get five new tunes ready.

His seat was in the middle of the hall. All the band members had to stand in a semi-circle in front of him.

Before placing the clarinet on his lips, he used to say a silent prayer, touch it to his head, and take a deep breath. That was a practice to prevent his asthma from surfacing once he started to play. And when he began, with his fingers with their chipped, striated nails flying over the keys and tone holes, asthma never used to trouble him.

The novices had to play the basic notes of Carnatic music at first. Then they moved on to the ragas. The initial lessons were over once they learnt to play the hymn 'Nanma Nerumamma' or the 'Mother Who Blesses'. When the clarinet was on his lips, Lazar asan controlled the class with his eyes alone. With his bloodshot eyes, he would glare at the ones who erred. Once the playing was over, the errant ones were sure to get a dressing down. Sometimes even a whack or two with the drumsticks of the side drums.

For other music bands, playing as they walked in processions was the main attraction. For the Devamata Music Band, performance was a ritual. In the middle of large grounds, a large double-sided drum as tall as the chest-height of an average man was stood on the ground. Like the shamans in primal worship, the members would stand in the orange light given off by flambeaus.

After the prelude was played, Cheruvilayil Johnson, the chief shaman, would make his entry with a chain flambeau in both hands, leaping and dancing and with an ear-splitting shriek. He was dressed in only cut-away trousers that came to his knees. His ebony torso would be glistening with sweat in the light of the flambeaus.

After his calisthenics with the two brands, he would play the big drum, swinging two flaming brands as mallets, made with cloth tied to two long ropes. He did it from a distance and then he did it closer to the drum, playing a demoniac, bloodthirsty beat. Clarinets accompanied this performance. Without missing a beat, he continued to play, contorting his body, leaping over the drum, lying supine on top of it, standing on his head and constantly moving. Leaping through fiery hoops, juggling with lit brands, and fire-breathing, he would keep up the drumming. The awestruck spectators would stand rooted to the ground, entranced by the ritual's mesmerizing spectacle.

Devamata Music Band was a performance group that Father Nickolaus had formed consciously by drawing upon the innate artistic traits of Karikkottakkarans. It was his design to maintain an artistic tradition that grew out of evenings spent around a firepan, playing the pipe, drumming, and singing songs after a hard day's labour. Lazar asan was summoned from Thiruvithamkoor. He was a consummate clarinet player who had been invited by swanky hotels and music councils for solo performances. Despite the promise of hefty fees, he could not soar into solos, breaking the chains created by the charm of the sounds of his accompanists. Lazar asan had conceived and choreographed the circus band performance in the light of the blazing flambeaus. Lazar asan's father, Manthacheraman, was a notorious sorcerer in Thiruvithamkoor, who practised shapeshifting and malevolent sorcery and who could snap a man like a twig, whence the name of its practitioners— *Otiyans* or those who snap people in two.

In all the church festivals of the valley, the main attraction was the Devamata Music Band's circus band event. Although blind, Marangan and Kapli were valued members of the band. Whether it was a stationary performance or a peripatetic one, Marangan would stay close to where his nose picked up the feminine odour. Assuming that anyone in front of him was a member of the fair sex, he had a constant, untiring smile on his face. Some of the girls would return the smile, believing his smile was directed at them. Although sightless, he would feel and sweep up those smiles.

Initially, I could not pick up his words. I started to pay more attention, assuming they were the argot of a blind person. They turned out to be the lewdest words I had heard about women's bodies and passion. As I expressed my astonishment, Marangan laughed aloud.

'I hope you didn't see that . . .' he asked innocently.

I became aware of the popularity of Marangan as a lover among the girls of the parish when I saw the youngest daughter of the lady cook sobbing in front of the padre.

He was consoling her, '*Molae*, both of your elder sisters have cried in front of me making the same demand. Didn't I, on that day, summon your family and warn all of you that he's a cad and not someone who should be allowed into your household? He won't marry any one of you. Even if he does, he'll untie the knot and flee sooner than later . . .'

After that incident too, I have seen women of all ages approach the padre citing Marangan. Some of them wept; others ranted; yet others confessed. Every time the padre summoned Marangan and questioned him, he winked and said, 'Which girl is that, Father? I can't recognize her. She must be lying.'

Much later, I realized that all the murmurs I had heard in the night between Marangan and Kapli were him narrating stories of his sexual exploits.

Chapter 8

Grandpa Chanchan

In 1965, the land that Father Nickolaus had initially bought unmeasured, on an estimated acreage from the landlord, was surveyed, demarcated, and registered in the name of Devamata Church. Thereafter, plots were measured out and registered in the name of each householder in the parish. Fourteen acres remained on record. In reality, it was close to twenty-five acres. Each Dalit who underwent baptism and joined the faith was given a plot from the balance, as decided by the general assembly. Gradually the land in the name of the church dwindled.

Seban's mother, Theyyamma chechi, and his sister, Bindu, had come to the vicarage to demand one acre of land in Karikkottakkary for her sister and children—who were then living on *poramboke* land in Ramakkal in Idukki—for converting to Christianity. Since the padre was busy, they came to me. She narrated to me the hardships her sister had to undergo after her husband deserted her. In order to survive and educate her children, settling down in Karikkottakkary was essential.

'It's doable. The church has enough land, and the padre is large-hearted enough to grant it. You can relax, Theyyamma chechi,' I reassured them.

When the padre was relatively free, I asked them to go to him. However, they kept sitting there, looking at me. Tears were dropping from her eyes.

'Why are you crying? Meet padre.' I was perplexed.

'*Monae*, Erani, this is not the main thing. My Seban . . .' her voice broke.

'What about Seban?' I too was worried now.

'Chettayi has moved out,' Bindu spoke now.

'Where to?'

'He's taken an old house on rent in Malom. He's living alone.'

'Monae, I've heard he's observing the period of abstinence for going to Sabarimala. And has worn the sacred beads as a mark of the vow.'

When Theyyamma chechi said that, I recalled that for some months I had not seen him at the church.

Bindu made things clearer, 'He left home stating that he wants to revert to our old caste.'

'If the padre comes to know of this, we too will be excommunicated We haven't told this to anyone.' I could sense the fear in her voice.

'Ah, nothing of that sort will happen. I shall visit him. Don't worry. After all, he's our old Seban.' I tried to console them in my own way.

I accompanied them to the padre's room. When he heard about her sister's tale, the padre said, 'The church is

running out of land. However, we cannot but help those in
need. Let them come and stay in your house for some days.
Let them attend the church and learn the liturgy. They must
also attend the retreat. Jesus will never forsake those who
want to be one with Him.'

Seban's mother was still upset when they were leaving.
At the time she was trying to win some land for her sister,
she may have been worried about what justifications she
could offer about her own son who was backsliding. She
may have been under the hope that I would be able to do
something to right the situation.

However, I could do precious little. I went twice to
Malom to meet Seban. I passed by my father's shop. Once
appan did see me. When I walked ahead as if I had not seen
him, his unblinking eyes were on me all the time. I felt
myself weakening inside. No, that won't happen!

Seban's was an old, thatched house. He kept it clean like
a hermitage. He was filling an earthen lamp with oil and
adjusting its wick when he saw me. He stood up.

'I know the only one who would come is you. Get in.'
He spread a grass mat.

'Why switch nests now?' I had nothing else to ask him.

'I'd told you of that sleight with achachan's caste
certificate. It's that I can return to my father's caste. I don't
need other benefits of Scheduled Castes. Merely the job
reservation, that alone. I can't survive without a job,' Seban
confessed.

'But for that, why did you have to leave your family?'

'There was no other go. KIRTADS will be doing an
inquiry into my application for a return to the Pulaya caste.
They need to be convinced that I am a practising Hindu.

If I live in a house which has the Sacred Heart of Jesus's image on the wall, tender coconut leaf crucifix, and where "Hark, Hark My Soul" is being sung, will I get the certificate, bro?'

I was staggered by Seban's practical thinking.

'Please make my folks understand somehow. I am now in the game of survival. Religion and such bunkum!'

Still in the black mundu that Sabarimala devotees wore during the period of abstinence and with holy ash on his forehead, he lit a beedi.

While I was leaving, he said this too, 'Don't call me Seban from now on. Sumesh Kumar. That's my name.'

I tried to make Sumesh Kumar's family understand. It did not matter to Vedikunjettan—Seban could do whatever he liked.

'Let him take care of himself. He's not a baby anymore,' Vedikunjettan said, stuffing his mouth with a wad of tobacco.

I looked at him; he was calm and pleasant. I had never seen his face otherwise. An imperturbable look was fixed on his face that neither hell nor high water could rattle. All that mattered to him was to render his karma well. Every day, hoe and pick in hand, he would be on the land tilling and nurturing it; on occasions, he would act as the chief butcher of swine; make firecrackers; carve idols on soap-stones; crack jokes; laugh. He ignored all the dark sides of life beyond these actions. He spoke nothing that would hurt anyone. If anyone said hurtful things, he acted as if he had not heard them. He faced life without measuring tools for sorrow. Gradually, life learnt to harmonize its own ways with Vedikunjettan's.

Theyyamma chechi was as accommodating and fluid as water. She took on the colour of the emotions that seized her for the moment. I was hesitant to inform her of Seban's experimentations. Therefore, I only told her that he was keeping well and that when the time came, he would be back with them.

However, I had a long chat with Bindu. She could understand his compulsions realistically. She seemed to accept her brother's battles with empathy. She asked me before we ended our conversation, 'Erani chettayi, aren't you getting involved to lighten my mother's grief? However, have you ever thought of your own mother?'

I had thought of her. Many times. All that time, what surfaced in my mind was the karma of an adulterous woman. And my avoiding her as the least of the punishments for bringing me into a life of endless humiliation. I did not have the heart to tell Bindu that.

On what was his last trip, Grandpa Chanchan arrived in Karikkottakkary during Christmas time that year. He got off the bus one day at high noon, dressed in a single mundu and a torthu used like a veshti. He had one change of clothes inside the plastic bag in his hand. He could have travelled the world in that fashion.

As soon as he disembarked, he squatted by the roadside. From there, in a loud voice that reached everyone present, he started to narrate the story of his travel.

'I left Paravur last evening. The train was packed with all kinds of blighters. I folded myself in a corner. Thereafter, taking one bus after the other, it's now noon when I have reached here.'

He sat in the sun for a long time. Though several men passed by him, he did not ask to be helped up. His own relatives—young men—were standing around in the nearby market. Since they knew his nature, none of them ventured to help him up. Eventually, when the lady-tailor Molamma was walking past, Grandpa Chanchan gave her an appraising look and said, 'Molae, help this granddad to sit down on the veranda of that store.'

Taking pity on the bent-over old-timer, Molamma gathered him up. With his arm around her shoulder, he got to his feet. As they walked towards the shop, Grandpa Chanchan asked, 'Are you new to this place?'

'Been here for two years,' Molamma replied.

'Looks like something is going to be sagging soon,' he said sorrowfully.

'I am holding you up, granddad,' she replied, tightening her hold around him.

'Oh, this granddad is talking about what's in his hands.'

Only then did she notice that his hand was pressing on her breasts. The spectators were grinning. She snapped back as if someone had spat on her face and shook him off as if something had stung her. Seated on the shop front, Grandpa Chanchan, watching her walk off in a huff, said gently, 'Molae, don't be cross with me. They ain't gonna sag this year anyway.'

He sat on the veranda for some more time and assessed the passers-by, finding out who they were and their provenance.

As he stumbled up the steps and into the restaurant, he said, 'Serve granddad lunch, he's famished.'

Thankan, the man who ran the restaurant, served him rice, his face showing no pleasure. As he was wolfing down big morsels of rice, granddad demanded, 'Do you have a couple of pieces of beef to spare?'

Thankan said, 'It's Lent, granddad.'

'What Lent do Pulayas observe, bloody son-of-a-gun convert?'

Thankan slammed the curry bucket on the table.

'Don't wiggle your dick! I am your real granddad. I have the right to tell you all this, you bounder.'

He had rights over every resident of Karikkottakkary. Most of the families were related to him. Even if not, he would claim and establish a relationship. He had the right to stay with any family in Karikkottakkary.

The next evening, I met him at Seban's home. He was having roasted and powdered pumpkin seeds mixed with jaggery and black coffee. I suddenly recalled the 'Pannikkalippattu' from a long time back—the old man who had sung it on my first visit to Karikkottakkary to watch the tug-of-war and taken his team to victory. He was no longer the same man. His hair had turned completely grey, he was hunched over, his skin was all wrinkles, and his teeth had fallen out. Only the soul that sustained the body had its old strength. It was burning perceptibly in his eyes.

'Who's this guy?' A gruff question.

'He's the secretary of the church,' Vedikunjettan said glibly.

'His family?' granddad pursued.

'They're from Malom,' Vedikunjettan continued to be evasive.

'From which family in Malom?' The question again.

Finally, I myself answered him, 'Adhikarathil family.'

'Ah, the Adhikarathil members are a mixed breed. But looking at you, you are a real Pulaya. Born to a Pulaya, too.'

'Will you shut up, granddad?' Bindu looked angry.

'Is he going to marry you, for you to get so testy?' he asked, pinching her cheek.

She found his touch repulsive.

'Monae, don't be bothered by this banter. Grandpa is just joking. I'll never allow this witch to be foisted on you.' He quickly turned jovial.

In the night, as we sat around the firepan under the mango tree, Grandpa sang. A song that was full of the infirmities and stumbles of old age. However, it held the promise and richness of a past age. It held the intoxication of unfulfilled lusts and desires in a life lived to the hilt for seventy-four years.

The bottle of hooch that had been opened for Grandpa, even though it was Lent, was placed near the firepan, still half full. I got to my feet, planning to leave for the church.

Grandpa said, 'Chanchan wants to meet that swine— your padre.'

I heard someone referring to Father Nickolaus so disrespectfully for the first time. I came away assuming it was mouthed by an inebriated old man. That night, the padre sent for me.

'He's come, has he, that Chanchan?' he asked me in despair.

'Yes, possibly he's come to celebrate Christmas,' I ventured.

'For him, there's no Christmas. He's lived a lifetime and he's yet to know Jesus Christ.' Padre bowed his head in sadness.

When I lay down to sleep, two old and wizened angels came near me. One had black wings and the other white wings. The black-winged angel held a burning torch in his hand; the white-winged one, a flashing silver cross. They led me to a cloud-covered room in which rain was falling. A naked girl was floating over drops of water. I kissed her nipples, which had drops of honey on them. She was Bindu. I woke up with that. There was a wet patch in the front of my mundu, shaped like a cloud.

On Christmas eve, when the carol groups had gone off to the different wards, I went for a stroll. I walked along the compound wall around the cemetery built using round laterite stones, now covered with slippery cushion moss. In the fast-dimming twilight, I saw Grandpa Chanchan seated in the middle of the cemetery. He was doing something on the ground.

'Grandpa . . .' I called out.

He turned around and when he saw it was me, he gestured to me to be silent. I went up to him.

On the ground, right in the middle of the cemetery, he had drawn a matrix using ash. In the cells of the matrix, blood-red hibiscus flowers had been scattered. On a spherical rock that had been placed in the middle, thick blood was dripping down. A headless black wild fowl lay by his side. Grandpa's eyes were shut. He was chanting something indistinctly. Finally, he plucked some wildflower from a plant next to him and threw it towards the stone and stood up.

'My forebears and progeny are lying here. They don't need crosses planted on their hearts; they need ritual sacrifices to be done. When I too reach there, my elders, who will give us the *kuruthi*?' Lamenting thus, he started to walk away.

'Grandpa . . .' I called him again.

'You are that padre's flunkey. The one who hates his own clan.'

He walked ahead and did not stop.

'I am a Pulaya. Born to a Pulaya.'

I said that to see if he would turn around and look. It worked. Grandpa stopped and turned around.

'Ah well, you know yourself. I had thought this place didn't have a bastard who has the courage to say this. Can you offer the kuruthi after my time? I doubt though; you'll still prefer to cling to the loincloth of that padre.'

'Father Nickolaus is a true saint.'

'Saint, *pthooo*,' he snapped, 'what the fuck has he done for anyone? He's the one who has tamed both swine and Pulayas. He knows that if he waves some food in front of both, they will follow him.' Grandpa was agitated and trembling with anger now.

'What's his fault? That he took them out of bondage?' I too was angry.

'How did they become slaves? Because they had a spine that they refused to remain straight. This Chanchan has been no man's slave all these years. Ayyankali rode the bullock cart everywhere. Not as a slave, but as a king. He knew our history. He knew we were kings who had ruled this country.'

'Which country did we rule?' This was history unknown to me.

'This Keralam. Even the name is ours. The land of Cheramans or Cheralam. The first kings of this land were us—Athiyan, Thithiyan, Antiran, Kindiran . . . haven't you heard this from your forefathers? The kings who planted trees and tilled the land. Who wore queen sago bead crowns on their heads. By bending our backs in front of all those who followed us, we became Pulayas. Who do you tell all this to? The mothers should tell their children who we are and were. The name Cheraman, or *cher'man* as everyone now prefers to say it, evokes scorn in every prick who hears it.'

I was astonished. This old man was narrating the history of the first Chera kingdom.

'If they hadn't followed him clutching their crosses, would your saint have given them even this rocky land? He made my children kneel before a foreign god. He shut up my forefathers in casks marked by crosses. He destroyed my clan. And yet he's a saint . . . phthoo . . .'

After hawking and spitting, when grandpa raised his head, he saw a statue-like figure at the cemetery entrance, its cassock billowing in the evening breeze and a biretta on its head—Father Nickolaus Sebaldus Braszio.

The padre chanted a line in Latin from the Vulgate, '*Tunc dicit ei Iesus vade Satanas scriptum est Dominum Deum tuum adorabis et illi soli servies.*' Then said Jesus to him, Away, Satan; for it is in the Writings, Give worship to the Lord your God and be his servant only.

Grandpa Chanchan hurried towards him and stood blocking his way. He may hurt the padre. I quickly moved to their side.

Grandpa Chanchan stared at Father Nickolaus with blazing eyes. History was dancing in his eyes. He stood there like a monument that bore witness to subjugation, bondage, despoiling of racial heritages and the entire past of the dark–skinned people.

Across him, with divine calmness, the padre countenanced a history that accosted the white man. His hands caressed the shoulders of Grandpa Chanchan with the gentleness of a soft breeze that had kissed flowers on the way. Knocking down the padre's arms and swearing, the helpless old man exited from the cemetery. The padre looked up at the sky and said a silent prayer.

'Eranimos,' he called at the end of the prayer.

'That Chanchan, who just left us, and I are the same— those who seek their godheads through different paths. There's no need to be fretting over whose is the right path. I believe that wiping the tears of the tearful is what's right. For another man that may be wrong. The many millennia of human life have proved insufficient to define what's right and wrong in reality. It will not happen in the hereafter, either.'

The padre walked towards the vicarage, serene as ever. During that year's Christmas too, with a calm, steadfast mind he led celebrations of the Holy Birth.

On 31 December, for the tug-of-war between humans to win a male buffalo, I sang the 'Pannikkalippattu'. From among the spectators, Grandpa Chanchan was cheering wildly. When I returned to the vicarage after the tug-of-war, the padre told me, 'Eranimos, you must go to Malom.'

'Why?' I was anxious.

'The paterfamilias of Adhikarathil is no more.'

Although the padre had advised me to go, I thought over it for a long time. Eventually, I decided that my going there would be better.

Sumesh Kumar—not Seban—accompanied me to Malom church. He described my grandfather's last days.

'He was not bedridden. The last few days he came out on the land, claiming that the crows were disturbing him. Then he went into the room and stayed in for five days. On the sixth day morning, he rose at 5 a.m. He was wearing only a torthu on his waist. He plucked a chandada leaf, made a cap from it, wore it on his head, and walked to the fields. He lay down on a wide, muddy ridge. All the family members arrived and called out to him; he didn't stir. When it was nine thirty, he asked Pyleechettan to fetch some water from the stream and drip-feed him. Realizing his death was imminent, the family members started to recite the Lord's Prayer. All those present claimed that he repeated it after them.'

What could have led the paterfamilias of the formidable Adhikarathil family to die on a muddy ridge clad only in a single torthu, after drinking water from the stream? I tried to console myself with the thought that it was an unknown fate.

The vicar at the funeral reminded us of it with his prayers, 'Remember you are dust and to dust you shall return.'

The size of the crowd for the funeral at Malom Church was unprecedented. All our relatives had turned up. I saw Emily chechi. She wore no ornaments except a steel chain and crucifix. She wore a high-neck blouse that covered her waist too and a sandal-coloured saree. She struggled to avoid looking at me. One of the nuns from the convent where she was studying was with her all the time.

Yielding to Sumesh's persuasion, I too planted a last kiss on the corpse. Amma looked at me with eyes that were overflowing copiously. Although I knew she was not grieving grandfather's demise, I turned my face away from her. I should get back to Karikkottakkary as soon as the funeral was over. As I walked out of the cemetery along with the others, I saw Grandpa Chanchan moving towards the open coffin leaning on Karikkottakkary Janu. Many other old-timers were present.

The tradition of serving cake and tea to the mourners after the funeral at the church started from that day. A baker was engaged to serve tea and a piece of cake wrapped in oil paper. More people than expected turned up. Tea had to be brewed many times. All the cake that had been brought was over in no time. The baker served laddoos instead.

Before he returned to Thiruvithamkoor, Grandpa Chanchan took leave from everyone in Karikkottakkary.

'Hereafter, Chanchan shall not come here to offer kuruthi. Someone should come there to offer kuruthi to Chanchan. If none of you come there of your own volition, our forebears will drag you all there, you misbegotten wretches.'

After Chanchan's departure, his predispositions kept troubling my mind. He was the one who had led me to look at Bindu—who, till then, I had looked upon as a sister—lustfully.

I invented reasons to visit their home. She was neither fair nor dark. With no blemishes, she shone like strained wild honey. Until a smiling Father Nickolaus, standing near the icon of Our Lady of Perpetual Succour, mentioned it, I had thought my desires and the frequent trips to her home were my own secret.

'Eranimos, I know you are heir to a property that is many times the size of this Karikkottakkary. That said, since you have decided to follow me, you need to have a mooring here. You require an unbreakable relationship with this land. I have set apart two acres of land for you. Build a house there; get married to someone you love.'

He knew everything. When I imagined my life with Bindu, I was thrilled.

Chapter 9

Ilanji Flowers

My grandmother could not come to the church to attend granddad's funeral. She was in the tharavad, seated in her room that stank of stale urine, trying to look for things dropped on the floor. Except for the fact that some things had been dropped on the floor, everything else had been wiped off her memory. She was locked up inside the room after she started to wander beyond the boundaries of the Adhikarathil lands, picking up all sorts of junk.

For her, that room became as expansive as the Adhikarathil estate. She took cover behind bushes in that space and excreted. The maids cursed and cleaned up after her. Her memories getting depleted day by day, with a shrunken brain, she lay on the four-poster bed like a withered leaf.

Another person who failed to turn up for the funeral was Sunny chettayi. After his wedding, he had moved abroad and returned only to attend the temporary vows

ceremony of Emily chechi, when as a novice she donned
the nun's habit.

The day after that ceremony, when I was waiting for the
bus at Karikkottakkary town, a red Maruti car drove up. As
the car slowed down to negotiate a pothole, I saw Sunny
chettayi in the passenger seat. His wife was driving. A little
girl in her nappies was on his lap, crying. When he saw me,
he asked his wife to stop the car. She muttered something
and speeded up instead. He put his head out of the window
and gesticulated that we would meet later.

He honoured his promise the next week. He came
in the evening. As soon as he got down from the car,
I realized he was no longer the proud, cock-of-the-walk,
fighting rooster who had strutted around his seraglio of
hens once. He had been turned into an effete broiler
cock, afraid to venture out of the coop, nay, even to stand
up and crow.

'We were headed to her house and in a hurry on that day.
We don't have much leave and we have to meet everyone,
eda. You don't go home, do you?' chettayi asked me.

'I'm constructing a house here. Father Nickolaus
prefers that.'

He proffered a State Express 555 cigarette and said,
'I hope you still smoke?'

'I stopped smoking after coming here,' I declined.

'Oh,' he stood leaning on the car and smoked. He
seemed to want to talk to me. I wished he would at least
laugh like old times.

'When coming from London I wished to gather our
old company and sit and chat. My daughter clings to me.

My wife thinks that if the baby gets close to her now, she will find it difficult to go to work when we return. It's true in a way.' He sighed deeply and said, 'Nothing can be done now.'

He was with me only till he finished the smoke. When he was leaving, he took my hand in his and said, 'You are a courageous fellow. You followed the path you chose. You have freedom. Everyone else in the Adhikarathil family is a prisoner. Undergoing a life sentence. We return next week. Be seeing you soon.'

Sunny chettayi was still downcast when he left.

Father Nickolaus broached the subject of a house blessing several times. After completing the construction, the house had been locked up. Vedikunjettan had supervised its construction. The black laterite, harder than granite, was blasted using black powder and used in building the foundation. Yellow-tinged stones were brought from Cheemeni, cut and shaped and used for building the walls. The ironwood tree that stood in the churchyard was cut down, plain sawn in Thyppadathu Cherian's sawmill and used by carpenter Rajan to make door and window frames. Kindal wood was used for the rafters and windowpanes. Roof tiles were brought from Valapattanam.

Three rooms and a kitchen. When the kitchen was being built, Bindu was present. The stove ledge should be at this height; the kitchen sink should be here; shelves should be at this height—she had opinions on everything. Vedikunjettan left the kitchen entirely to her discretion.

Nelthare wood was used for the chords and cashew wood planks nailed in as floorboards of the attic. Red ochre was used to polish the floor. Only the kitchen area was tiled. Sumesh Kumar paid a visit when the house was nearly complete. He was elated. He liked the house. That he wanted to meet his family made me happy too.

As we entered the house, Theyyamma chechi turned her face away. The radiance on Sumesh's face was not dimmed by the rejection. Vedikunjettan, as was his wont, smiled and continued to peel areca nut. Bindu ran to him and held his hand. Sitting at the feet of his father, Sumesh pulled out a paper from his pocket.

'Achacha, I have achieved the objective of moving out of the home. I have got a job, a government job as a clerk in the Irrigation Department. This here is the appointment order.'

'Smart fellow.' Kunjettan complimented him and read the order.

In an unexpected move, Theyyamma chechi came rushing. Wiping her hands on the seat of her mundu, she grabbed the order off Kunjettan and looked at it wide-eyed as if she were watching a movie. She then hugged her son. Bindu ran her fingers through his hair.

The happiness I had witnessed in that house many years ago had returned. Theyyamma chechi killed and prepared a chicken. The aroma of fried coriander and chillies carried the news to the neighbours—this was the house of Karikkottakkary's first government employee.

After the meal, when Sumesh took leave, Theyyamma chechi said peremptorily, 'You are going nowhere. This is your house. This is where you shall stay.'

'That's not possible, Amma. I got this job out of the reservation quota for Hindu Pulayas. To keep the job too, it has to stay that way. How can I live here as a Christian?'

The reality that he presented through that question defeated Theyyamma chechi.

'Will your becoming a government employee stop you from being our son?' That was a mother's logic.

'Amma, please don't worry. In a couple of years, I shall build a house somewhere away from Karikkottakkary, and we shall have a decent life there.'

When Sumesh stated his plan, Theyyamma chechi was mollified to some extent. Yet she persisted, 'Till then you can live here . . .?'

'No, don't do anything that may put your job at risk. There'll be no one here to offer you another.' Kunjettan, who had been keeping quiet, spoke up in his sincerity.

Theyyamma chechi seemed to believe that everything would fall into place in two years. When we left, Kunjettan accompanied us. After walking in silence for some distance, he stopped suddenly.

'Seban, this is something that you do know. Your father was born in Thiruvithamkoor. As the son of a dark-skinned Pulaya. And grew up too as a Pulaya, grappling with mud and muck and living in a hut. I realized that I am also a human being for the first time after I came here, to this Karikkottakkary. It's in the shadow of this crucifix that I stood tall and with my head unbowed. Therefore, I don't plan to leave this place for any other. You should build a house, have a good life. Your achachan will sit here, imagine you living a good life in your own house and celebrate. And when I die, you shall bury me under the cross. Monae, you may go now with a happy mind.'

Kunjettan had grown and spread like a tree beyond my reach. When he left us, Sumesh was conflicted, and his strained face showed it.

His first posting was to the Thayyeni office of the Tejaswini Irrigation Project. The department had employee quarters in Thayyeni and after three months, he was allotted one. Sumesh told me his work was best suited to slouches. During monsoons no one needed irrigation. So, there was no work. During summers, there was no water to send down the canals. The entire office could relax then too. His main job was to prepare the salary slips of the five officers and handle correspondence relating to their service issues. If some funds for maintenance work were released occasionally, the assistant engineer and the contractors decided the split. Sumesh spent most of his time idling in the office and the quarters.

After a month in Thayyeni, he called me. 'You should come here tomorrow. It's something very important to me. I have only you to tell this.'

His quarters, built of granite, were on the hill above the smaller dam and stood among tall trees. The windows were painted green. The lamp posts on the street were corroded. Beyond the mini compound wall of the quarters, a derelict park could be seen. The untrimmed hedges, overgrown grass and moss-covered animal figurines gave it a wild, unruly beauty.

Seated on the corroded steel benches, we gazed across the reservoir. A white fog was descending on the water like angels.

'Erani, do you recall our Vimalagiri College days?'

'No, for me now Vimalagiri College is essentially you, you alone. I have nothing to remember about it anymore.' I was being truthful.

'For me, it is not so. There hasn't been a day I haven't thought of the college after leaving it. From the day I was branded as a Karikkottakkaran there, I swore to myself that I would do something. Every breath I have taken till this time has been only to achieve that.'

He was speaking like he was someone else.

'I know, your objective was to land a job, even by forsaking your family, your faith. It was the right decision.' I had no doubts about his objective.

'The job was only the way to the objective. The objective was something else altogether. A lovely one.'

The shaft of twilight that seeped through a break in the fog turned his hairless cheeks bronze.

'Don't be shocked. Tomorrow my objective will be fulfilled. You should be the first witness.' He took my hands in his and beseeched me.

'Please make things clear, eda,' I too pleaded.

'At first, I thought her eyes reflected the disdain she had towards dark-skinned people. The most beautiful, high-born and pedigreed among the progeny of the Christian overlords. I swore to myself that she would become the wife of this Pulaya. Thereafter all my prayers, efforts and endeavours were to win her over.'

'Who is she?' I couldn't contain the suspense any longer.

'Think back. The most beautiful girl among our college mates. You also adored her.'

'Soumya C. Chacko,' I whispered.

'Yes. I got close to her so that I could trample on her haughtiness. However, she wanted to be shorn of the trappings and baggage of her lineage and her complexion, fed up with her family's grandstanding. She started to love me to take them on. Erani, a woman's heart is not what we see it as. I can say with certitude that no Pulaya woman will love me as much, will undergo as many sacrifices as she will. Tomorrow, she will come to the registrar's office leaving behind everyone dear to her. The marriage will be registered at the Thayyeni Sub-Registrar Office. You should be with me as my everyone.'

I thought of the sketch he had drawn of Soumya. So, in that, she was looking at him and not me.

'You win. You have brought life around to where you want it to be.'

I looked at Sumesh who glowed dark in the reddish glow of the setting sun. Every one of the billions that pass through the world is as big as the universe. Their minds have dreams vaster than the skies. Determinations more steadfast than mountains. Hopes that remain kindled till the end of the world . . . unhealed wounds . . . vengeance . . . self-realization. Every human being is a universe in himself or herself.

'Sumesh, will it take place tomorrow for sure?' Doubts still lingered in me.

'Of course, it will. She was ready to elope with me a long time ago. I was holding her back. I needed a job. She was the one who suggested reverting to the Scheduled Caste status.'

Everything happened as he had predicted. She was determined; her steps assured and firm. When she signed the register, I looked at her face. It showed the gratification of succeeding in doing what she had set out to do.

When she was told of Sumesh's wedding, Bindu looked appalled.

'Hey, look, sister-in-law rivalry,' I teased her.

Her mind was far too lost in thoughts for my stab at humour to penetrate it.

Theyyamma *chedathi* kicked up a furore and then slowly simmered down. Kunjettan smiled with his usual equanimity.

Most of the Karikkottakkary families were beneficiaries of the foreign-aid maternal and child health or MCH programmes. With the advent of those programmes, the food distribution scheme of the church gained wider acceptance. The cornflour, soyabean oil, and broken wheat were distributed with the help of the government. Every parish had to nominate an MCH volunteer. A decent sum was paid as an honorarium.

Father Nickolaus told me, 'I have identified Bindu as our volunteer.'

The MCH office was adjacent to the catechism class office. After she was made the volunteer, she was found in that room most of the time. In front of her room stood an ilanji tree. When she had free time, she would pick its fallen flowers and make garlands. A garland could always be found lying on her table. And its mild fragrance lingered in the room.

If she was there, I always ensured that I went into the room only in the company of Father Nickolaus. Once, when we were seated in her room, someone came to the vicarage to meet the padre and he excused himself.

With him leaving, I started to make errors in the accounts I was writing in the ledger. As I took up the safety razor blade to scratch out the incorrect entry, like a starry-eyed lover I asked Bindu, 'Did you like *our* house?'

Although she stopped with, 'It is a good house . . .' it seemed to me as if she wanted to say more. I looked into her eyes. She too was gazing at me. After a little while, she said, 'I like you, Erani chettayi, a lot. Everyone wants our marriage to happen. Do you also want it that way?'

I was elated beyond reason. She had opened up about something that had been suffocating me all this while. While I was trying to decide the apt phrases for my response, she continued, 'If your reply is a "yes", chettayi should forgive me. Perhaps no one will understand what I am saying. I felt most proud of my Seban chettayi when he left home to go back to being a Pulaya. Without accepting the handouts that a religion had to offer and live in ignominy, he chose to leave with dignity. However, I was devastated when I came to know that it was all part of his exertions for the sake of a fair-skinned Christian girl.'

I was getting jittery about where this conversation was headed.

'Erani chettayi, do you know every human being in this Karikkottakkary yearns to be a Pulaya? It's out of their desperation, and only their desperation, that they remain Christians. And I work for the church. To marry a Christian and live here labelled as a convert is not what I would like to do. I want to bring up at least my children as Pulayas. Bounden to no one; slave to nothing or nobody, free Pulayas. That is why I don't want you as my husband.'

She lay her head on the desk and started to weep. Although I wanted to reach out and comfort her, my broken heart had turned me numb, making any movement impossible.

That night, I stood at the window, gripping its bars and gazing out. I could see the ilanji tree that stood in front of Bindu's office. It would have been older than I was. Leaves, flowers, branches, the trunk with thin bark, roots . . . my roots . . . *chee* . . . I was thinking about the ilanji tree to keep from thinking about my own roots. All thoughts swivelled back to me.

What am I?

God . . . *who* is my God? Forefathers whose thirst is slaked by the blood of black fowl spilt on sacrificial rock? Or the taste of flour that dissolves on my tongue in the shape of a sanctified white disc? Who *is* my God?

Why this life?

Offspring of an illicit relationship, living as a parasite in a noble family, uncounted as a member of any clan, humiliated—how far was this life going to drag me on? Who would give me a lineage to drive my roots into? Which womb would be the receptacle for my seeds?

The Womb! The answer lay in the Womb!

After spending a sleepless night, in the morning I climbed Sultan Hill, and I screamed into the Womb.

'Yonacha, climb out. I need answers.' My voice echoed inside the cavern. As my eyes adjusted to the darkness, I could see it was empty.

Parting the lemongrass bushes, I ran to the cave in the valley. I stood at the opening and shouted, 'Yonacha . . .'

Along with the echoes of my own voice, the stench of rotting flesh reached me. I entered the cave. The movement in the stagnant air caused by my entry made the reek insufferable. As the gloom inside the cave thinned out, I saw the carcass of a bloated, rotting boar.

As I moved closer, I saw that its limbs were long like a human's. Swine and humans are all the same. There was a boulder near the animal's head. I saw clotted blood on it. Next to it was a sheaf of black fowl feathers with ants swarming over it. I looked at the boar's head. Mankuruni Yonachan . . . My illicit father.

For hours I sat near the corpse of the man who had passed away without giving me my answers. Should I inform people, have a post-mortem done and bury him in the cemetery?

The light that reached through the cave opening showed the fowl's blood on the stones. A Pulaya had died. For him where is the world after death? The Pulayanar Kotta in which his forefathers live accepting kuruthis? Or the Kingdom of the Father that opens after sanctification by St Peter?

The sacrificial stone provided the answer. Till someone else came along, he would be interred here. I went out and sealed the cave opening with a big boulder.

When I reached my room, it looked like a strange place to me. Someone else's place. Someone else's things. Nothing was mine. I sat down on the bare floor. Later, without realizing it, I lay down. Karikkottakkary was a fort. A fort on which a cross had been erected. A fort bound by magic.

The gates of the fort opened. The old wizard was standing at the portals.

Father Nickolaus Sebaldus Braszio.

'Monae, Eranimos,' he called out in a plaintive voice.

'Father, I want to confess.' For some reason, that is what I said.

'Come,' he called me gently.

The padre sat in the confessional with his head bowed.

'Father, why did you come here? Why did you confine these innocent people—who believed in gods that lived in their fields, loam, stones, plants and deceased forebears—in this church along with these lifeless clay idols? Why did you destroy a culture by cutting it off from its patrimony, beliefs, biological relationships?'

In the face of my onslaught, Father Nickolaus did not quail; my hurricane did not make him sway.

'My son, I have already spoken to you about rights and wrongs. I have only one answer to all your questions.' He sighed once and said, 'Because my God asked me to.'

He blessed me, took off the stole worn during confessions, and rose to his feet. He knelt in front of the altar and spread his arms.

That night, after spilling the blood of a black fowl at the opening of the Sultan Cave, I bid goodbye to Karikkottakkary.

Chapter 10

Veluthachan

The land in Karikkottakkary is black; at Vettakkal, it's all white. Karikkottakkary is made up of rock-hard, sunburnt, abrasive laterite. Vettakal has the softness of sugary sand, cooled by the sea breeze. Karikkottakkary is torrid, with its parched, cracked ground hiding water deep in its nethermost regions. At Vettakal even a finger-deep hole will have dancing wavelets lapping inside it.

Lazar asan told me that Yonachan—whose family name was Cherakkudi—hailed from somewhere near the Arthunkal church in the Alappuzha district. I did not inform him of Yonachan's death. Lazar asan had stopped visiting him after Yonachan had stopped his moonshine business. He had taken his custom to the new moonshine makers in the Kodagu forests.

I reached Arthunkal and made inquiries. No one had heard of that family. When my inquiries gave me no lead at all, I started to wonder what next. Exhausted from my efforts to track the family down, I was lying on the sand in the Arthunkal churchyard.

To be honest with myself, what was I searching for? The roots of someone who I imagined could be my father? A tenuous relationship that had only infamy as its base. After I found out about him, where would that leave me? What good would it do to me?

If the result of my findings was not going to change my life, what was this possibly infructuous search in aid of? The more I thought about it, a few justifications started to form in my mind. Other than this search, what else was there for me to go on with? There was no question of a return to Karikkottakkary or Malom. My objective was to prove my Pulaya roots. For what? For a girl who wanted to give birth only to children of a Pulaya? How much of a tragedy is it that my life should be circumscribed by such a fatuous pursuit?

Night had fallen. The sea breeze came in caressing the dark waves. The church yard was deserted. A sodium vapour lamp was burning atop the cross, painting the granite stones of the compound wall yellow. I was alone on the sand amid the footprints of the people who had come with their novenas, supplications, and prayers of gratitude during the day.

Suddenly, the breeze grew stronger. The spray from the high waves that rose in the wind had woken me up. Was I sleeping to be woken up? When I looked towards the church, the sea was roaring in through the portals.

Breathless, I was drowning in the sea water that had appeared all around me. As I was slipping into the depths of the sea, exhausted from my efforts to stay afloat, a sailboat came into view, flying Cheraman Perumal's flag. There was a radiance on board. Hands of light reached out from the boat and pulled me out of the waters and into the boat. I recognized the radiance.

'Arthunkal Veluthachan!' I joined my hands worshipfully.

'I have become hoary listening to the deceitful supplicants of many generations. I was shiny dark as the deep sea. I am Cheran Senguttavan, the one who, from the mountains to the sea, infused power into the dark skin and is the bearer of the Dravidian might.'

The locks of the king turned into waves. The *kuttavan* who lagged the sea. Yellow light cast patterns on the fort of the Adi Chera fitted with the cross.

'Great Lord, please give me an answer,' I cried and pleaded, believing that I was the subject of a king.

'Aren't the heartthrobs that pass through our linked hands our kingdom's language rather than prayers and commandments? What then is the need for kings and vassals?' The star-studded crown of night jiggled on his head.

'I still haven't got an answer,' I wept.

'Your clan, right?' The king pondered.

'You are my son. Heir to the kingdom bordered by the sea and the mountains. The crested floating-heart flowers that adorn the hairs of the blue nymph; the laurel tree that feeds your hunger with pollen, fruits and cooling juice; the jasmine that encompasses the forest's darkness which provides the sanctuary for plants, animals and birds; the devil's tree that wears the crown of thorns; the kurinji flowers of the high castles set aflame by the golden arms of the sun—all belong to you.' Believing everything belonged to him, the Chera king spread his arms to indicate the vastness of his realm.

'Nothing, I have none of that. One who is ostracized, who is shorn of traditions and heritage, who has no mate or companion, unaware of which god should he invoke . . . I am orphaned.' I plummeted down like a bird with broken wings.

The Chera king shook his head in negation of everything I had said and laughed. The ripples of his laughter caused waves in the sea. The sailboat started to rock. The waves climbed over our heads and over the mast. Clutching the short hairs of the waves, I dived to the bottom. I spat out the salty sand that was filling my mouth and took deep breaths.

'Monae.'

When I opened my eyes, Father Nickolaus was standing over me.

'Father,' I squawked.

'Get up, why are you lying on this sand?' He tried to help me up.

It was not Father Nickolaus. It was some other priest. It was daybreak. The Chera king's fort was blocking the sun. I sat with my head down for a little while. I spoke resolutely, firm in my belief that I still had an objective to achieve.

'Father, I have come from Malabar in search of someone. I fell asleep out of exhaustion.'

'Whom do you want to meet?'

'I want to meet a karanavar from the Cherakkudi family.'

'Cherakkudi?' he mulled over the name. 'As far as I can recall, there is no such family in this parish. Our accountant will know. You get up and have some food.'

The accountant arrived around 9 a.m. He was older than the priest. He wore square-rimmed glasses. Only one eye of his moved; the other eye seemed to be made of glass. He cocked his head and took a long look at me.

'Cherakkudi . . . they aren't Christians, are they? They are Pulayas.'

'Yes, they are,' I agreed.

'They are from Vettakkal. There are several families. I don't know the names of anyone there.'

With his head still cocked, he proceeded to the office.

Vettakkal was to the south of Andhakaranazhi. There were more water bodies than land. It had shrimp farms separated by bunds with sluice gates. I was seeing for the first time a place where visiting a neighbour meant a boat trip. The stench of the coconut husk steeped in the water was nauseating.

I put my question to a woman who emerged from the water with a bundle of the blackened, rotted husk.

'This place is full of people from the Cherakkudi family. Whom do you want to meet?'

Whom do I want to meet? I asked myself the question.

'Don't you know the name of the person?' Dropping down and rolling the bundle of husk, the woman asked again.

'I am coming from a place called Karikkottakkary in Malabar . . .' Before I could say anything more, she spoke as if she knew what was required.

Switching over effortlessly to the elided dialect of North Malabar, she said, 'You're from Karikkottakkary? Your man's been here for the last three-four days,' and then called out loudly, '*Edi*, Kunjolae, Kunjolae . . .'

Who is the one from Karikkottakkary, I wondered.

When the adolescent Kunjole emerged, the woman instructed her, 'There's that karanavar at Kannamma's place. Take this man to that house.'

The girl walked ahead; I followed. We crossed a small causeway made with the sugary sand. Now the houses were close together. Every house had a fence with tapioca trunks as stakes and woven coconut thatches strung together between the stakes. Standing at the stile of a house the girl called out, 'Kannamma chechi, is grand-uncle here? Someone's here to see him.'

Kannamma came out on to the veranda of the hut. She was around forty years old. Her clothes and hair looked dishevelled. The girl seemed to find something funny, laughed and ran away.

'What are you grinning about?' Kannamma took umbrage at the girl's impudence. 'Young man, you come in.' The invitation to me was cordial.

'Where are you coming from?' she asked, tying up her hair.

Although they had started to sag, she had huge breasts.

'From Karikkottakkary,' I replied.

'If he's from Karikkottakkary, then he must be Eranimos. Send him in.' I was astonished when I heard Grandpa Chanchan's command.

Had I come in search of this man? Was someone leading me on without me knowing of it?

He was lying on a large charpoy which used gunny strips in place of ropes. He was not wearing his single mundu; it was lazily thrown over his waist. His hands were placed over his head with the fingers intertwined.

'Eda, couldn't you have come at a *better* time? Ah . . . it's okay,' Grandpa Chanchan laughed.

I sat down on a cane chair near the charpoy.

'I knew you would come . . . the only wonder is, how come you landed up here. I was expecting you at Paravur,' he said as if everything had been anticipated.

'I don't know how. I have reached here is all I know.'

'How does that play out? Edi Kannammae, help me into a sitting position.' The old man seemed to be weaker than before.

'Coming,' she said from the kitchen. However, she took her own time to come.

While helping Grandpa Chanchan into a sitting position, she asked me, 'Shall I make some coffee for you? There's no milk though.'

'No, I had some tea already.'

As he was being helped up, grandpa's roving hands had gone in search of some crevice or the other.

'Arrgghh . . . this spavined bull will not leave one in peace,' she raged.

'It's one of Chanchan's pranks, my girl,' he laughed.

'And you'll do your pranks in front of strangers?' Kannamma chechi explained her indignation.

'Ah, don't you set your eyes on him now! He is already been spoken for; there's a sweet girl in Karikkottakkary,' Grandpa Chanchan said, to rile her.

After a little while, he came out of the house, leaning on his stick. He sat on the veranda outside for a little while, lost in thought.

'You have left behind everything and come here, have you? But what is there to do here?'

I had no answer to give him.

'You are strong and healthy. A Pulaya who has a healthy body can live anywhere.' He himself provided the answer to his own question.

'Kannamma, from today onwards please provide a mat for him in the ante-room. You'll profit from it, surely.'

The mat that was spread for me led me to a new life. I took up the hoe and pick for the first time in my life. I got down to getting my hands dirty. The soil in Vettakkal was rich and loamy. Everything I planted grew luxuriantly. Wondrous growth. My labours were for the benefit of fair-skinned landowners. During harvest, they whispered among themselves, 'Look at the Pulaya's golden touch.'

Not long after I reached Vettakkal, I asked Grandpa Chanchan about Yonachan.

'Cherakkudi is our family name. Yonachan's mother, Chennila, is from this family. Chennila was cohabiting with an Ezhava from Ambalappuzha. Yonachan was the offspring of that relationship. Would an Ezhava keep a Pulaya woman for long? After he left her, she, along with her son, accompanied your karanavar Kuncheriya to Malabar.'

So, I had Ezhava blood too in me? I was not fazed by this new knowledge. Cheran Senguttavan's laughter at the Arthunkal basilica gave me strength.

One late evening, four months after my arrival in Vettakkal, bhajans were being sung in the houses in the neighbourhood, after the ritual of lighting a brass lamp called *nilavilakku*. Grandpa Chanchan sat on the veranda, abusing and berating everyone.

'You whores, where do Pulayas have nilavilakku in their culture? Rama, Rama . . . who's this fellow? The forebears of Pulayas had names such as Aathan, Aayi, Aathi and so on. Chant those names, if you must, you sluts.'

This abuse-filled diatribe was a daily occurrence. After that day's performance, as he sat basking next to the firepan in the yard, the sound of a bicycle bell was heard.

'Now who is that parading himself on a cycle?' Grandpa Chanchan demanded, peering into the dark with his poor sight.

'It's me, Marangan.' He emerged into the light, walking stick in hand.

'Ah-ha, you have arrived? All the women around this place better wear cast-iron chastity belts. The blind rake has come.' Grandpa laughed aloud.

Marangan remained mute. No laughter out of him. He groped and found his way to the veranda of the hut and sat down.

'How come you have nothing insolent to say?' Discomfited by Marangan's silence, Grandpa Chanchan prodded.

'Grandpa, Father Nickolaus has left us . . .'

His quavering words, as I emerged from the pond, froze me. I expected Grandpa to laugh uproariously.

'WHAT . . .?' Grandpa Chanchan looked up at the heavens.

'It happened last Friday. Saturday was the burial.' Marangan started to cry loudly.

Grandpa Chanchan kept gazing at the house. The firewood that had become damp in the mist was hissing, smoking and exploding occasionally.

'My children, Karikkottakkary will be destroyed.' I heard Grandpa Chanchan's portentous comment in the darkness amidst the smoke and sparks.

Marangan described the last days of what was a legendary life. He had experienced the padre's death through the splintered, broken and wailing voices.

'After Eranimos's departure, he had been rather silent. On the previous Sunday, the week before his death, during the mass he spoke for an extraordinarily long time. Some of it was about his own life. The rest was the history of Karikkottakkary. After the mass, the people wondered why he was talking about all that then. Did anyone imagine it would be his last speech? He collapsed on Tuesday. On Wednesday and Thursday, day and night, the whole parish was present in the churchyard, wailing and praying. Father was conscious. On Friday morning, he sought everyone's forgiveness. Who knows why that god-like man sought forgiveness . . .

'At ten o'clock, the prelate from Kannur arrived and gave him the Last Sacrament and Holy Communion. After the prayers, Father Nickolaus pointed towards the almirah. There was a small boulder inside it. The bishop said that it had been taken from Mount Golgotha. That was placed near Father's head. At noon, some things were recited in Latin. After that, I heard only loud wails from the people . . .'

Unable to say anything further, Marangan sat all hunched up.

'Nicolae, you beat me to it.' The words rose like flames from the firepan.

After some time, Marangan took up his narration again.

'When the news of his death spread, there was a constant flow of people into Karikkottakkary. No one knows from where so many people had come. The parishioners remained in the church precincts even after the burial. They sat there the whole night, singing dirges.

'On Sunday, the new vicar and bishop arrived. There was a public meeting. The bishop gave a eulogy on Father Nickolaus and listed his good deeds one after the other. At the end, he said one more thing. That the church and other institutions in Karikkottakkary would be under the direct control of the diocese. Everyone clapped and passed the motion.

'From that Monday, the new priest started his reign. The vicarage was swept clean and turned inside out. Father Nickolaus's bed, vestments and everything else were taken out and burnt. The rooms were repainted. I had requested that his stuff shouldn't be burnt. Aren't they holy relics?'

Marangan could not continue. I held his hand. He lifted his head. From his rheum-filled hollow eyes, there was a surge of tears.

'Erani, stating that the days of the Father of Swine were over, the vicar let out all the pigs. They were grunting and running helter-skelter around Karikkottakkary, not knowing where to go. They were taken away by some people. Kapli and I asked the priest what we should do. He asked us if we had homes; when we told him we had none, he said that there was an orphanage for the blind in Sullia and he could drop us there. He said the Church could not assume any more liabilities. Before leaving for Sullia, hugging me, Kapli cried a lot.'

Marangan did not speak after that. I recalled the two of them, sleeping like twins in each other's arms. Now they were children who had lost their father. Father Nickolaus was father to a whole region.

None of us slept that night. On the veranda, Marangan sat facing the yard. In the anteroom, I lay on the mat, staring at the ceiling. On the charpoy inside, Grandpa Chanchan lay contemplating his past. Kannamma was on the floor sleepless, worried about the other three sleepless orphans.

The next morning, Grandpa Chanchan rose from the bed by himself, leaning on his stick. Propped up by his staff, he walked along the row of slanted coconut palms to the other end of the bund.

On the far side, an old, gnarled red cotton tree stood at the shore of the lagoon. Poison nut plants had covered the base of the tree. Grandpa Chanchan used his staff to part the plants. There were pebbles beneath the tree. He removed the dried leaves and red cotton flowers lying on top of the stones.

Kannamma chechi came with a plantain leaf with tender coconut, paddy grains, and hibiscus flowers on it and asked me to hand it over to Grandpa. She looked towards the cotton tree and placed her hand over her heart. When I reached there, Grandpa was sitting down, leaning on his staff. He gestured to me to sit.

He started to sing an indistinct threnody in a very slow, drawn-out tempo. While singing, he picked up the paddy and threw them at the stones. He followed that by taking out, one by one, petals of the hibiscus and throwing them on the stones. After flinging the last petal, he fell towards the stones in a swoon.

He went beyond this living world. He went to the other world of his forefathers and talked to them. When he got back to our world, his eyes were brimming with tears. He got up and drew a cross on one of the stones. He placed the tender coconut in front of the stone.

He held my hand when we came out from beneath the red cotton tree. As we walked on the bund, he started to mutter.

'It's an old story. My father Vellon was the head Pulaya at the Kainakkari fields. Our life was like that of the Mupli beetles of Karikkottakkary. During the day we would be steeped in the slush of the paddy fields. At night, in the light of a firepan, we would create a roof of some sort using thatches and curl up. When I had enough strength to hold the hoe, my father asked me to join in the work. I had decided I wouldn't do bonded labour. Appan made it clear someone who would not work was needed neither in the family nor in the clan.

'I left my family and siblings behind and fled. I travelled during the nights. In the daytime, I hid myself in the forests. Running through the nights, I reached Paravur, and collapsed at the kitchen door of an unknown house.

'In the morning, someone woke me up and gave me water to drink. It was the house of an Ezhava called Ayyappan. For him, there was no pollution distance to be maintained. He gave me gruel; gave me a place to sleep; he hugged me and said that I was a brother to him. The people of that place called him Sahodaran, or brother. That good man taught me to read and write. He also got me the job of a mail runner between Paravur and Kochi.'

It was no debilitated old man standing in front of me using the strength of his staff; it was the king who had accumulated within him all the strengths of the Pulaya clan. Cheraman Chanchan Senguttavan. I realized a new respect for this man, absent till then, was budding inside me.

'Those days, a Pulaya being the mail runner was a funny business. If a high-caste Hindu was travelling on the same route, the mail runner had to hide himself in the jungle on either side of the path. Most of the time, it was by crawling through paddy fields and stooping behind bushes that I could reach Kochi. To go a distance of eight miles, I'd have to do sixteen.

'One day, a procession of Nampoothiris was headed to the *vaara sadya*, the free temple meals served to brahmins after vedic recitation on full moon days. I had hidden myself behind a copse. A hand fell on my shoulder; a question in broken Malayalam followed—"Aren't you the mail runner? Don't you have to reach the mail bag in time?" When I looked up, it was a white priest. I stepped back, claiming that I hadn't broken the taboo of untouchability by touching him. The priest claimed that he did not believe in pollution or untouchability. After some thought, he took out a devotional scapular and put it around my neck. He said that now I could go anywhere I wanted. A dog, a cat or a Christian could take any route . . . I was getting to see the proper road for the first time. I ran with my head held high. Even when Nampoothiris and Nairs were brushing past me, they didn't ask me to move away. Nickolaus's magical scapular opened the way for me. When I took in hand the belled spear of the mail-runner, I would wear the scapular around my neck. When I kept down the spear, I took off the scapular too. I never addressed Nickolaus as Father. I had someone to call father, didn't I?

'To wear clothes and to walk around freely, many Pulayas started to wear the scapular. However, giving into the exhortations of some mindless priests, they also cleared groves where we worshipped serpents; felled our guardian trees; tossed our memorial stones into the sea. In place of our songs of worship, they sang hymns of the Holy Father and the Son. I could not stomach it. The only priest I knew was Nickolaus. I went and showered abuses on him. I threw my scapular at his feet. He stood smiling all through it. From that day, I started to run without the scapular, and no one stopped me.

'When he took Pulayas en masse to Malabar, I swore at him again. Again, he only smiled. He told me one thing— for him, our karanavars and Jesus Christ were the same. I only came to know yesterday that he had taken one of our memorial stones with him. However much I would abuse him at Karikkottakkary, all he did was stand and smile.'

Recalling that smile, Grandpa Chanchan took a breather, stopped walking, and sat down. He turned to me and said, 'He held on to his God for dear life till his last breath. Wasn't it our duty also to embrace the gods of our land . . .?'

He did not speak after that. In his helplessness to distinguish between right and wrong in the complexities set forth by the races for all of the eighty-one years of his life, he hobbled towards our home.

Chapter 11

Pulayanar Maniamma

Kannamma chechi was as black as the night. On some nights, Marangan would enter the house from his usual place on the veranda. Marangan and Kannamma chechi would become one with the night. During the movements of the dark night, the hisses and moans of Kannamma chechi, who had never learnt to hold them back in, would rise like the chanting of mantras.

From the charpoy, Grandpa Chanchan would say, 'It's a pleasure to sleep with these sounds in the background.'

I had thought of her as a village prostitute who had become isolated. That night, two people arrived under the cover of darkness. Two Nairs from Chengannur. They had come to buy coir mats. She opened the door, spread a mat for them on the veranda and told them, 'Lords, please sit down.'

After chewing the paan, the seated lords conveyed their need.

She laughed when she heard their wish.

'I don't give my body to anyone for money. When I feel the need for it, I will get whoever is at hand to do it for me. You lords have come at the right time. Today I feel the need for it.'

'That is good. So where is the mat being spread?' The lords were in a hurry.

'There's no need to spread any mat. Do you know what I need today? I will invite a few people. In front of them, you shall . . .'

What she said then was something no woman would have stated with such supreme vulgarity.

'For some time now, I have been wanting some Nairs to do that to me.'

'You fucking whore, what did you say?' The Nairs jumped up.

Pulling out a sickle from the rafters of the hut, she too leapt to her feet.

'Yes, I am a Pulachi . . . the queen of Pulayanar Fort. I will have whomever I want come here. I will get him to do whatever I want. Loosen your loincloths, you misbegotten whoremongers. This Pulachi is not going to lie down for you to stick your pricks into me. You shall lie down for me. I will summon all the people and show them how you lick my pussy clean. I shall show you what is a Pulaya woman.'

As I looked through the gap in the thatch door of my anteroom, I saw both the Nairs had prostrated themselves at her feet.

'We need nothing. Please let us leave with our dignity intact,' they pleaded.

'Do what she wants to be done to her,' Grandpa Chanchan started his hectoring from inside the hut.

Raised sickle in hand, Kannamma chechi stood with her foot on the heads of the recumbent Nairs—as the embodiment of lust, as an incarnation of Devi, as Pulayanar Maniyamma. I recalled that Bindu, when she expressed her desire to be mother to a Pulaya's children, had the same look on her face. After that episode, when she had obliterated the serfdom of an entire race by exercising personal independence and agency over her own body, I never thought of Kannamma chechi as a harlot.

Although she had invited me often with 'Whenever you feel like doing it, *eda* come to me, no one has said that Pulayas should hold it in', I never took her up on it.

'I don't repress my desires and torment my mind. Our body is our salvation, our god, our everything . . . denying, starving it is the real sin.'

She was giving out ancient philosophy. Philosophy as old as the ur-Pulayas. She and Grandpa Chanchan lived as per that philosophy.

Kannamma chechi was married to Kariyan Pulaya from Thuravoor. Although everyone in the vicinity had converted, Kariyan's family held fast. There was a reason too. His house was on the western boundary of the Thuravoor temple. They were devout Pulayas for two generations before him. They worshipped the presiding deity, Devi, daily, standing at a non-polluting distance from the temple wall.

After the Temple Entry Proclamation that allowed the *avarnas* to enter temples, their day began with a visit to the temple and prayers to the deity. Kannamma was accepted into the family as the maid of the Thuravooramma, their

deity. She, on her part, did not pay heed to the existence
of such a temple. Her in-laws resented that and started a
whisper campaign against her.

'Does she have her monthly periods round the year?
When she refuses to worship and sing the bhajans, she
should not forget that her daily route takes her past the deity.'

His family told Kariyan to control the Pulachi he had
wed and get her to obey him. Every day late in the evenings,
when he heard his mother's exhortation, he would decide
that he would crush her arrogance that very night. However,
in the night, on the mat in their anteroom, the Pulachi held
the upper hand and lorded over him. He stayed meek with
his head bowed, as he watched her swagger. Clutching his
long, curly hair, she led him on, along the contours and
curves she wanted him to follow. After such journeys, spent,
as they lay down, she would tell him, 'This is our worship,
our pooja. Our temple, the deity, the sanctum sanctorum,
everything is this. Now you tell me, should I go to any
other temple?'

'No, Kannamma, what does my amma know of
anything?' Kariyan would tell her submissively. The next
morning, when he saw the temple, his regrets would start.

'Ammae, Devi, I had gone along only because my
Pulachi said it. This innocent simpleton may be forgiven.'

Unlike other Pulaya women, Kannamma chechi refused
to go to the fields. She built an enclosure and started to
breed goats. She built a coop and reared hens. In the sliver
of land beyond their yard, she planted tapioca and plantains.
When she had spare time after tending to her goats, poultry
and plants, she went to the seashore and gathered mussels,
caught fish and sold them to the toddy shop. She earned

plenty of money. When they saw her making money hand over fist, her mother-in-law and sisters-in-law stopped their griping.

One late evening after the monsoon season, Kannamma chechi made a fire pit in the yard. She sat near the fire pit, let her hair down and basked in the warmth. Her mother-in-law and sisters-in-law sidled up to the fire pit. Kariyan also quickly joined them. Soon there was a ring of people around the fire pit. Their neighbours too wandered in.

The fire and the audience made her break out into songs—songs none of them had heard; songs that were only within her. Her singing made her family and others in the audience look at her in wonderment. The men among them gawked at Kannamma. Their women rolled their eyes at them without others noticing it. After that, they never came to warm themselves at the fire pit.

Kannamma's fire pit was smouldering all the time. The tubers of the tapioca planted before monsoons were dug up and roasted in the fire. Fish caught from the stream was smoked on the fire pit. Together they were eaten with salt and bird's eye chillies. When their bellies were full, the mother-in-law and the sisters-in-law went inside and slept.

When the mother-in-law woke up during the night and peeped through the holes in the thatch, she espied a resplendent Thuravooramma seated near the fire pit. Her devotee Kariyan was prostrate before her. The deity had his curly locks in her hand and was being worshipped.

When the mother-in-law rose in the morning, she found her son and daughter-in-law sprawled near the fire pit scandalously déshabillé. She hawked, spat out and shrieked, 'Get up and clear off, you hussy.'

Kannamma smiled. Kariyan wept.

The deity had appeared at night in a vision. She had pronounced that she was annoyed. She demanded atonement and propitiation. Since it was the period of abstinence for visiting the Sabarimala shrine, Kariyan's mother advised him to wear a string of tulsi beads and practise the prescribed abstinence. After praying at the Thuravoor temple, he wore black mundu and beads.

Kariyan was made to sleep alone in the anteroom. Kannamma was to sleep with her mother-in-law.

'Everyone in the house must practise abstinence,' the mother-in-law decreed.

In marked contravention of the rules of abstinence that prescribed only vegetarian food, the next day too Kannamma prepared the fire pit, roasted tapioca and fish and consumed them. None of the others came to warm themselves at the fire.

For four days she lay beside her mother-in-law. On the fifth day, straight after the basking at the fire pit, more inflamed and incandescent than the fire, she barged into the anteroom.

The next morning, his penance having been vitiated the previous night, Kariyan cried and told his mother, 'I don't want her, amma. She's Neeli, Kalliyankkattu Neeli.' Neeli, the legendary, vengeful yakshi who used to seduce, kill and eat men.

Kannamma laughed.

'I am no Malikappurathamma. When you feel like having me, you shall come to where I am. When the day comes when no devotees come to me, I shall return and remarry you.'

Kannama was referring to the beautiful woman who emerged from the body of a demoness killed by Lord Ayyappa. She asked Lord Ayyappa to marry her. He promised her that he would, the day any first-time devotee stopped coming to worship him. She became a symbol of eternal wait by a woman for her man.

Kannamma never returned from Vettakkal.

'She is a genuine Pulaya woman, one who has royal blood in her,' Grandpa Chanchan said. 'Our forefathers were strong and bold like her. They ruled the land, pure Dravidians. We lost all the glory when interbreeding started.'

Grandpa would say all this to no one in particular. After the monsoons started, he prattled on, all the time. As he was unburdening all that had entered his mind in his eighty-nine years, all its contents flowed out from him in a steady stream.

'It's after the blasted Aryans arrived along the western coastline that we become denigrated and degraded; we were told that our clan was no good and our complexion was inferior. They came only to graze their cattle. Along their route, they built temples. Since our lands were forests and jungles, they didn't bring their women with them. Much like the first batch of Christians who migrated to Malabar.

'When they reached, they found we were already there—when I say we, I mean the indigenous Pulaya, Paraya, Pullon, Vetton, Karimpalan, Kurichyan, Paniyan, Arayan, Kosavan, Ulladan and hundreds of other tribes. Each area had its tribe. The Aryans slept with women of every tribe. The children born of these liaisons were tall and fair. The buggers kept these children with them and dubbed them as

Shudras. All the Kurups and Nairs of this land came from them. Which means all these overlords of today were born from our land and our women.'

History lay brimming in Grandpa Chanchan's eyes. Occasionally, a couple of drops fell on to the grey hairs of his beard and disappeared. He kept up the narration all day and night. Their chronicles, stories, humiliations, battles, surrenders—everything that marked the life of the indigenous people stood out in them.

One late evening, when the sky was thick with dark rain clouds, he stopped talking. He lay on the charpoy, staring at the ceiling. He fell asleep sometime in the night. At midnight the rains roared in from every direction. He woke up with a start. Kannamma chechi went in and covered him properly with a blanket.

'Eranimos,' he called softly. 'For the last so many years, I have been searching. I have travelled all over Kerala to discover if there is a genuine Pulaya left here. I couldn't find one. Everyone had been corralled. Inside churches and temples. A Pulaya is not one who lives inside; he lives in the open. Our gods live in the open—the open land, open skies, open air are the shrines where they reside. You don't go in.'

While the rains kept lashing down, he did not say anything more.

It rained the whole night. All the rivers that ran from the east breached their banks. When the sun rose, the lagoon, the fields, and the land were one unbroken sheet of water. The blanket lay crumpled on Grandpa Chanchan's bed. We walked around as far as we could go, calling out to him. Marangan sat on the veranda, whimpering.

When the water reached the yard and rose to the floor of the hut, I felt something graze my ankle. When I picked it up, it appeared to be a smooth piece of wood.

It was Grandpa Chanchan's staff.

The waters receded only after two days. The root of the red cotton tree was full of slush. On the third day, when it was possible to walk over the bund, Kannamma chechi handed over to me the stuff needed for kuruthi. I walked up to the red cotton tree and offered kuruthi for Grandpa Chanchan.

Though many months passed, no one asked after him. Everyone had forgotten that such a man had lived among us. Only Kannamma chechi would remind me on every new moon day about the kuruthi. He who had travelled the whole length of Kerala had passed on without leaving even a footprint behind as if he had walked on water all the while?

'Doesn't he have any children?' I asked Kannamma chechi a question that I had not asked him.

'He has many, in various places. But their legal fathers will be someone else. I know one person who is definitely his son. My husband Kariyan.'

She said this without displaying any emotion.

'Shouldn't we be informing him . . .?'

'It doesn't matter whether he knows of it or not.' Kannamma chechi ended the conversation there.

Everyone in that place celebrates the feast of Veluthachan of Arthunkal Basilica. It runs for ten days from 18 January. On the ninth day, a procession with a float of a royal chariot drawn by four white horses in its vanguard is taken out. Veluthachan, riding that chariot, proceeds to the seashore with thousands of devotees as his entourage. In the inky darkness of the night, he gazes across the seas. I always felt the sea and the kuttavan who lagged the sea were standing face to face. The sighs of centuries were crashing on the shore as waves. The king was conveying his gratitude to the sea that had granted him the land to reside in. The place, or *alam*, that joined the chernna or sea is *cheralam*. Multiple etymologies . . . multiple beliefs . . . multiple faiths . . . Our history is painfully fragile.

Standing away from the crowd, I looked at Veluthachan's face. He looked sad. The light from every candle whitened him. The saint who turned fairer and fairer and became someone else. Veluthachan . . . Senguttavan . . . Grandpa Chanchan . . . Father Nickolaus . . . Riddles of blackness and whiteness.

When I was leaving for the feast, Kannamma chechi asked me, 'Your Christian pong hasn't left you, has it?'

'Only what's inside the church belongs to the Christians. What takes place outside are Pulayas' celebrations. The crowds, the chendas, the cheering, the colours—all that is ours, ours alone,' I said, smiling.

'Umm . . . you can go. Feasts and festivals are for people to watch and in which to parade themselves.'

The procession was on its way back. A disappointed Veluthachan was borne inside. The music band set and chenda ensemble were reaching a crescendo. The sky was filled with colourful and ear-shattering fireworks. The finale was thousands of metres of crackers strung together, interspersed with *amattu*s or high-decibel, rocket-fired mortars. It went on for over ten minutes. The whole area was enveloped in thick acrid smoke. At the end was a volley of amattus. After that, there was a momentary silence. And then everyone broke out in full-throated cheers—an amalgam of relief and happiness.

Everyone was waiting for the smoke to clear to start leaving for their homes. As the smoke ahead of me thinned out, the form of a man bent with old age emerged. He placed his hand on my shoulder. I peered at the man's face.

Adhikarathil Philippose boss!

'Monae Eranimos,' he called with a quivering voice.

He was so weak that he could have collapsed. That was the only reason we took him with us.

'Who's this?' Kannamma chechi asked.

'Adhikarathil Philippose boss.'

'No, this guy's father,' he corrected me.

I laughed. He seemed to be living in the past. I was giving someone who had come for the feast a place to sleep for a night. I did not think of it as anything more than that.

'Where to now?' I asked him the next morning.

'That's for you to decide. I have been wandering in search of you for the last so many months. Then I had this thought that I might find you at Veluthachan's. To be blessed with you, hadn't your mother and I come to this Veluthachan at first?'

Admittedly, I had that connection with Veluthachan.

'Why were you looking for me?' I asked.

'To inform you that your mother is no more.'

'Oh,' I said carelessly and looked away.

'Monae, I won't blame you. It couldn't have happened any differently. Time always takes us back. It's just that all of us—you, me, your mother were mere victims.'

When I looked at him askance, he met my eyes with a level gaze.

'I should have told you this long ago. The only reason I didn't was because everyone feared that the reputation of our family would be sullied.'

'What?' I felt a twinge of suspense.

'The real history of our family.'

He became breathless. He blew on the black coffee that Kannamma chechi had served, and continued, 'The recorded history of Adhikarathil family is a big lie. A figment of M.P. Padmanabha Panicker's imagination; a crock of lies. Fables that our forebear Varkeyavira had told us. There was no Adhikarathil family before his time. We bought with money everything that we wanted—chronology, history, pedigree, lineage, nobility, positions in the Church, everything. Wherever the family took roots we were the biggest donors to the Church and the society. In aid of what? To impress on others that we were not Pulayas; and to convince ourselves.'

I was unable to understand what he was driving at.

'Great-Grandad Varkeyavira was subjected to humiliation. He fled from the people who had enslaved him using his race; he absconded from his own heritage and people. He started a new life in a new place. He was a Pulaya before he made the break with his past. His real name was Mada, one of the two sons of Cherakkudi Aadi.'

I was astonished as I watched Cherakkudi segueing into Adhikarathil.

'Grandpa Chanchan?'

'One of the members of Cherakkudi who didn't convert and remained as Pulayas. Aadi, the progenitor, was a slave of a high-caste *thirumulppadu* from Kollam. Karimpan and Mada were his sons. When they grew up, Mada wanted to marry a fair-complexioned girl. Karimpan ridiculed him—where was a slave going to find a fair maiden? Mada had a devious plan for that. During one of the *pulappedi* days—when Pulayas were allowed to walk out in the open, and if Pulayas threw any projectile that touched high-caste women seen outside their manors, the women would be polluted and expelled from the family—he flung a stick at a girl from a Nampoothiri tharavad.

'With the fair maiden won that way, he fled the place. He reached Uzhavoor, got baptized, and became a convert. Karimpan continued life as a Pulaya. He had three sons—Vellon, Chathan, Thandan. Chanchan is the son of Vellon, the uncle who got separated from me three generations ago,' he concluded.

It was becoming clear to me why this history of the Adhikarathil family was kept away from me. I felt that my research was coming to a satisfactory conclusion.

'There are questions for which I still have no answers. There are raw wounds. What do you have to say?' I posed it as a challenge to him.

'Son, your wounds may still heal. But there is a woman who has bled a painful, agonized death from wounds that never healed for years together—your mother. You should, at least, come to her grave. The answers to all your questions can be found there. I have come here only to tell you all this.'

When he was leaving, he turned around and said, 'I can give you the answer to one of your questions. It is the truth, and it is the only truth. I am indeed your father.'

He said nothing more. He walked over the bund towards the road. I stood there as if I had been struck by lightning. Then, despite myself, I called out, 'Appa.'

He had gone beyond the point where my brittle voice could have been heard. I shut out all my thoughts. Every one of them was headed for my jugular like misdirected, whirling urumis.

I was at a stage where I had forgotten everything. My sojourn in a new place had brought me into a new life. Why did he have to come now to drag me back to old battlefields and graveyards?

He could be lying. But those words . . . those words were not lies. No human can lie with such conviction, such sincerity. If that was true, then my mother . . . as my head was beginning to explode on that pyre, Kannamma chechi called me.

'Eranimos, come.' She invited me to sit beside her on the cow-dung floor.

I should say I keeled over more than I sat down. Like a small child, I sat leaning on her body. She hugged me indulgently and kissed my forehead.

'Monae, I have not delivered a child. I have not experienced a mother's feelings. However, as a woman, I call tell you that no mother can bear her own son rejecting his paternity.' She poured agony instead of soothing balm over me.

'Let me tell you one more thing. Irrespective of the enormity of the pain that a child causes, a mother can forgive him for the simple reason that he is her own child.' She kissed me again on my forehead as a seal of the authenticity of her words.

'Amma,' I said.

That day, for the first time, I pressed myself against her breasts. I could feel those barren breasts yielding milk, wetting my hands.

Chapter 12

The Third Chera Empire

The cold season was ending. Tender leaves were breaking out on the rubber trees. Bunches of tender cashew nuts festooned the cashew trees. I was standing in front of the renovated cemetery of the Malom church that had only now planted shrubs and trees. A huge arch above the gate declared it to be the Garden of Resurrection.

Leaves from the tall mahogany trees next to the cemetery wall, which had shot up without spreading out, had fallen on the tombs. Tombs were laid out on either side of the centre path of the cemetery. On the right were family vaults that could be bought for money. On the left were the graves for the public. The first family vault in Malom cemetery belonged to the Adhikarathil family, where my great-granddad, Kuncheriya, was buried. Both my grandparents were buried in the same vault. The last body to reach the vault was my mother's.

On the wall of the Adhikarathil bungalow, photos of my smiling, laughing mother could be seen, all taken before my birth. From the time I could remember, her eyes were always bloodshot and swollen. Had I taken my mother from a life of laughter to a life of tears? These thoughts flooded my mind as I stood before the crypt.

I had no prayers to offer.

Appan was waiting outside the cemetery.

He had a look of gratification on his face that he could achieve at least this much. When he saw I was leaving the cemetery, he came towards me and gathered my hands in his own. His body was radiating heat as if from a fire pit.

'I was the one who broke up our family,' appan said as if he was apologizing to me. 'Do you recall your grandfather passing on the presidency of the church to me? The candle falling from his hands and setting fire to the vicar's vestments was not without reason. He saw Chanchan, who was standing in the crowd, and you at the same instance. His hands shook when he had the vision that the Pulayahood that had been shunned by his forefather was coming back to haunt us.

'That day, he made me swear upon the Bible that even if I had lost you, I would never reveal our family's secrets.'

Appan walked out and sat down on the platform under the mahogany tree. He made me sit beside him.

'If I had disclosed to you at that time how you were born dark-skinned, you wouldn't have had to wander around in this fashion. You wouldn't have hated your own mother like this . . .'

He could not continue. He sat with his head bowed for some time.

Then, shaking his head as if to throw off the words that had congealed in his brain, he started to talk again, wanting to be rid of them, 'You will recall me telling you that Cherakkudi Mada, that is Great-Granddad Varkeyavira's Pulaya brother Karimpan, had three sons—Vellon, Chathan and Thandan. Thandan ran away and surfaced in Thudanganad and got converted. I named you Eranimos after the name he had chosen for his own christening.

'Your mother's father, Rarichan, is that Eranimos's son. Like we had chosen Adhikarathil as our family name, Vallyath was chosen by Eranimos as his family name. Both have devolved from the Cherakkudi family. The norm that our forefathers had laid down that alliances should be chosen after checking at least five generations was followed to avoid instances such as this. My father broke the norms of our tharavad by getting me married in haste. We came to know everything after our wedding. You inherited your dark skin because cousins, a few times removed, from Cherakkudi family had got married and you were our offspring. Son . . . you are not a bastard, and your mother is not a fallen woman.'

Appan had broken down completely by the time he said this. I was looking over the cemetery's wall at my mother's tomb. The cross stuck out of it like the handle of a sword that had been thrust into the very heart of the tomb. That handle bore the indelible fingerprints of only one person— me. I rubbed my hands together.

I recalled the blood I had spilt on the sacrificial stone in front of the Sultan Cave.

'Yonachan . . .?' I asked with suspicion.

'Also of the Cherakkudi stock. Thandan's older brother, Chathan, had many daughters. An Ezhava had taken advantage of one of them and got her pregnant. When he brought that woman Chennila and her son to Malabar, Granddad Kuncheriya didn't know they were family. Yonachan, her son, was a good worker. My father discovered that they were from our family after the death of Granddad Kuncheriya. That same day, my father dismissed him and exiled him from Malom. Everyone stopped you from going to Karikkottakkary because Yonachan was there. However much we try to hide things, that which should get revealed will be revealed.'

My appan's face showed relief. I placed my hand on his shoulder. Suddenly, he hugged me close. It was the first time in my life he was doing that, at least in my memory. As we stood like that, I felt that if I had hugged him at least once, I would have recognized that he was my father.

He stroked my head and consoled me.

'Monae, we can't erase the smell and colour of the soil from which we have sprung, no matter how many generations we pass through. We are victims of a mistake that Granddad Varkeyavira had made without realizing this home truth. You have corrected that wrong with your own life. There is no need for you to cry any longer.'

The Pietà in front of the church had been cleaned and repainted. The essence of that sculpture is the sufferance of a mother who transcends the death of her own son on the cross. I fancied that the Jesus lying on that mother's lap was dark-skinned, had curly hair and thick lips. A fair-complexioned mother holding a Pulaya son on her lap. Hail the mother to all Pulayas!

Another face arose in my mind—of one who was waiting to give birth to Pulaya children. At Karikkottakkary.

The new Karikkottakkary was growling. Echoing off the mountains around it, it turned into an intimidating booming sound. Red smoke and rumbling sounds were emitted as if from a volcano. The roads to Karikkottakkary were full of trucks loaded with laterite stones or proceeding to load them.

Karikkottakkary looked like another planet. On either side of the road were flag posts, festoons and installations of the Communist Party. Only those looked neat. The trees, plants, buildings, workers were all covered in red dust and looked inanimate.

Stone-cutting machines were roaring inside the large quarries among high mounds. Where new quarries were planned, earth-moving equipment was flattening the ground. Only the machines were moving. The people in between them had been obliterated by the dust in the air. Nothing green was left behind in Karikkottakkary. The places where houses stood had been turned into quarries. The few houses that remained were like isolated memorials, for the people who once lived in them, hoisted on small square towers that stood in deep pits. No one seemed to be living in them.

Of the five wells that Father Nickolaus had got made for the drinking water project, three had disappeared. Although the remaining two stood like square towers, they held no water. Since Karikkottakkary was now uninhabited, there was no more need for drinking water schemes.

The stones were being cut using circular blades attached to the sides of mechanical tillers. To make sure the blades cut true, nails were driven into the ground, strings pulled between them and lines drawn along them. There were small earth movers suitable for the removal of broken stones, clods and loose earth.

The largest quarry was on the land owned by the church. The once-white church now looked ochre red, covered in dust. Only the land on which the church stood was left to quarry. The school had been closed, as there were no students. The cooperative bank had been liquidated. All the institutions built by Father Nickolaus had been destroyed.

When I got down from the bus at Karikkottakkary, it took some time for the church to be seen through the pall of dust. In a corner was a statue. When I went close, I saw that it was a ruthless posthumous distortion of Father Nickolaus. I saw no one familiar to me; everyone had sold their properties and moved away. The Communist Party had made it known that Father Nickolaus had bought land in Karikkottakkary contravening the provisions of the Land Reform Act, and all the title deeds issued in Karikkottakkary would be rescinded. This meant that the quarry owners got the land for a pittance.

All the commercial establishments too had closed down. All that remained were two restaurants, a grocery shop and a repair shop for the stone-cutting machinery. When the saw-toothed blades that resembled Lord Vishnu's Sudarshana Chakra were being sharpened, sparks flew off them. Unrepairable, rusted machinery had been junked and were lying around.

Although I could see Vedikunjettan's house from a distance, I had to take many detours to reach there. I climbed the steps that had been cut into the side to reach the house from the deep quarry. Kunjettan was seated on the veranda. Both his feet were bandaged and, from the look of it, infected and oozing pus. There was no expression on his face though he was looking towards me.

'Kunjettaaa . . .' I called out to him.

Before he could answer me, Sumesh emerged saying, 'Appan is blind.' When he saw me, he expostulated, 'Erani . . .' and then fell silent.

'Is that Eranimos?' Kunjettan queried.

'Yes,' I replied.

'Are you able to see me?' Kunjettan asked, labouring under the impression that the whole world was in darkness.

'Yes.'

'Oh, so all of you can see?' he asked, a tad disappointed.

With sagging pillars, the thatch suffering hair fall, and wrinkled and cracking walls, the house had become an old hag with little life left in her. Through the door that looked like a gap in the hag's teeth, Theyyamma chechi emerged.

'Oh, it's you, son, where have you been all these years?'

'In Thiruvithamkoor, with Grandpa Chanchan.' I did not elaborate.

Pushing a plastic chair towards me, Sumesh said, '*Eda*, sit down.'

'When he heard of Father Nickolaus's death, Grandpa Chanchan said that Karikkottakkary is finished. I realize how true it was only today when I see it here,' I addressed Sumesh.

'As long as he was alive, Karikkottakkary had only one decision in every matter—his decision. After his passing, everyone had the liberty to make his or her own decisions. For themselves. But it's not possible to make faultless decisions.' Sumesh was expressionless when he said that.

'Didn't you go to your office today?' I asked.

'There's no need to go every day.'

He kept looking at his father's sightless eyes. Theyyamma chechi said something and started to weep.

'Can you please shut up, amma?' Sumesh said, showing extreme annoyance. Theyyamma chechi got up and went inside.

Sumesh wore a shirt and ordered me, 'Come with me.' As we were leaving, Kunjettan started to sing:

Alas and alack, our good neighbours,
Our house has been burgled.
One is a darkie, one is a whitey,
Another is stout and strong.

Although Sumesh turned back and threw him a dirty look, since Kunjettan could not see it, he continued to sing.

As we walked along the ridges between the quarries, I looked in the direction of the Sultan Hill. It did not look as if something like that had ever existed there.

'Has everything including the cave been hacked out?' I asked.

'The first place they cut up with their machines was the cave,' Sumesh said as if he did not care anymore.

We reached the house that Father Nickolaus had built for me. That plot of land was also a quarry now.

'If they see an unoccupied land, they'll get in and start hacking. No point now talking about it,' Sumesh said because he felt that I may have had misgivings about who would have permitted them to quarry on my land.

The roof had sagged like a withered plantain leaf on the verge of falling off. The plaster on the walls was cracked and had fallen off in many places. Termites had completely eaten up the doors and windows.

Sitting down below a chandada tree that had grown near the house, Sumesh said, 'Squat. There's a lot to tell you.'

I sat down with questions bubbling up inside me.

Seated in the ruins of a land that literally had its roots slashed, from what he said, this was what I could gather.

Life in Thayyeni was wonderful. A charming place, a charming relationship. However, Soumya wanted to move to where her relatives lived. So, Sumesh requested for a transfer to a place near her home.

After a while, her relatives started to turn overtly sympathetic. The sympathy that the high-born feels towards the low-born. Poor fellow, how much he had to struggle to get a job. Sumesh does not have the street smarts to compete with cunning people. Her family kept harping on everything—his incapacity to earn well, to manage his own affairs, even to father a child.

When Soumya started echoing such sentiments, it became insufferable for Sumesh. When it was apparent that he would not be able to sustain it any longer, he decided to divorce her.

After his narration, he sat with his head bowed. His posture made me suspect that he was still deeply in love with Soumya C. Chacko.

'You have a job. So, it's not that it's all come to an end.' I grasped his hand.

'Hmm . . . maybe things will be okay. I'm building a new house in Blal. I shall take appan and amma there. I'm not sure if appan will be alive by the time the house is completed.'

'What's wrong with him?' I asked.

'He has diabetes. His kidneys have also started to fail. He is surviving because twice a week he is taken to Kannur for dialysis.'

We remained silent for a while. I then asked him the question that I had been wanting to ask all the while.

'Where's Bindu?'

Sumesh raised his head and looked at me. I wondered if I had made a gaffe by asking the question.

'I had thought you would marry her. Soumya told me that you had decided against it because she is a converted Christian. In a way, that's a good thing. Whatever revolution you may talk of, those who are not compatible shouldn't marry. I know what I've gone through.'

Maybe he was reliving those memories; Sumesh was silent for a while.

'Compatibility was not the reason it did not happen.' I did not elaborate on it. Perhaps he sensed there was something he did not know. He did not dwell on it and continued his conversation.

'You remember Robin who was in the Devamata band? He married Bindu. He left her within a week of their wedding. After that, she got a job in an NGO. Their focus is on Wayanad. She said she was going there. After that, we did not hear from her for a long time. When the quarrying started in Karikkottakkary, she came with some people and started an agitation against it. The people here got together and swore at her. Our neighbours asked appan why he couldn't control his daughter. We hear that she is in Wayanad now.

'Those who are still here have now been saying that if we had backed her then this land wouldn't have been laid waste like this. Her name appears in news reports once in a while. What she's doing is the right thing. I only thought about myself.'

We sat gazing at the sky screened out by the dust. Dusk was falling and the machines had fallen silent and were parked at the back of the quarries. Like mobile terracotta statuary, workers moved towards the tube wells.

We reminisced about the old times. The Karikkottakkary that had formed our lives was no longer in existence. The quarry pits may get filled. Vegetation may be replanted. However, whoever comes later will never believe that this land was different. Like any other land, some lives with no roots will float over this land too and pass along. Nothing more.

'From now on, I shall be in Malom. You must call me,' I told him when we parted.

The Adhikarathil tharavad had become like a serpent grove. Once in a while, someone would come and sweep and clean the house. All the workers had left us. Appan was having his food from restaurants. Some days, he would sleep in the shop. The estates were all overrun by wild vegetation.

My parents' room was filled with deathly silence. In the past, my mother's voice was hardly heard from the room. On the nights when appan would scold her, she used to cry silently. I realized only now that appan was angry with her for hiding her antecedents, her family's origins. Because the forefathers had chosen to hide their roots, she was the victim of a racial riot in the bedroom.

The kitchen where Emily chechi and I were caught in flagrante delicto lay silent. She was really my sister. Was that incestuous Maundy Thursday night the most sinful of my nights? After having met Kannamma chechi such thoughts should not have arisen in me.

Appan told me that Emily chechi had left the convent and got married. The liberation of one's own body, its agency, is the highest independence. I felt respect for her. She had not surrendered her agency over her own body fearing the calumny of leaving the convent. That was good. Let Emily chechi turn into Devi Kannamma.

When I started to decay inside the decrepit tharavad of ours, one day I set out of the house. The estates were overrun by Siam weed and mimosa thorn. The air was still and cicadas and birds were chirping. Crows were busy making their nests on the rubber trees.

It was the season when the tender leaves of the rubber matured. Sunlight fell on the ground through the canopy dappling the ground. A haldu tree that had shot up from a clump of rocks was towering over the rubber trees. I sat down on the rocks beneath the haldu tree. Small saplings were trying to find the sun from beneath the baneful shade thrown by the rubber trees. They may survive and thrive over the years.

I closed my eyes. A breeze that only the mind could perceive blew across me. Nature enveloped and subsumed me; the movement of the worms underground; a few had surfaced and were crawling over the fallen leaves; gold-coloured beetles; spherical beetles with rainbow exoskeletons; caterpillars with dotted mantles; earthworms; millipedes; snails that leave gooey trails; scorpions; centipedes; snakes with their heads in the air; hares; mongooses; toddy cats; squirrels; foxes; wolves; deer; leopards . . . wildfowl, crows, greater coucals, peacocks, and bats that fly over them . . . creatures abounded on the ground, in the vegetation, in the sky. And me, one among them. For years, I was in search of this serenity.

I started to walk to the end of this forest. The climb towards the east had started. How is it that all the trees are in bloom so early? When I reached the summit of a hill, I could see smoke rising from the rocks below. Looking closely, I realized it was the mist rising from the waterfall. I started to walk down towards the waterfall.

The water was flowing down soundlessly. The fog had reduced visibility around me. Were there deer on the other end of the pool? As I drew closer, I saw they were not animal movements, but men and women dressed in black.

One of them leapt into the water. The dark form swam underwater like a black fish towards me. When it was close to the bank, it even looked like a mermaid.

The mermaid who rose from the water resembled Bindu. Water dripping off her, she was walking towards the shore. She was wearing no clothes. I was also standing naked.

Bindu laughed. Seductively. Her laughter set off sprays of water.

'It's going to rain. Are you going to lie here?'

I opened my eyes, hearing my appan's question. I was lying on the rock in our estate.

'Eda, rubber prices are going up. We can't leave this place like this, going wild. I have asked Sabu to bring some Bengalis who know the work.'

When appan was saying this, I was still drowsy. I shall decide what is to be done after I wake up.

Scan QR code to access the
Penguin Random House India website